Praise for *Ella Unleashed*

· · · · · · · · · · · · · ·

"Readers will laugh and cheer as Ella jumps through hoops to get the perfect date for her father."
—*SLJ*

"Realistic and sympathetic, with an appealing protagonist and an interesting hobby for texture."
—*Kirkus Reviews*

"Cherry incorporates realistic depictions of angst, friendship, love, and internet safety into this middle-grade family drama, but she also adds humor in events beyond Ella's control." —*Booklist*

Check out these other books by Alison Cherry!

Ella
UNLEASHED

BY ALISON CHERRY

Aladdin

NEW YORK LONDON TORONTO SYDNEY NEW DELHI

ALADDIN

An imprint of Simon & Schuster Children's Publishing Division

1230 Avenue of the Americas, New York, New York 10020

First Aladdin paperback edition September 2019

Text copyright © 2018 by Alison Cherry

Cover illustration copyright © 2018 by Angela Li

Also available in an Aladdin hardcover edition.

All rights reserved, including the right of reproduction in whole or in part in any form.

ALADDIN and related logo are registered trademarks of Simon & Schuster, Inc.

For information about special discounts for bulk purchases, please contact Simon & Schuster Special Sales at 1-866-506-1949 or business@simonandschuster.com.

The Simon & Schuster Speakers Bureau can bring authors to your live event. For more information or to book an event contact the Simon & Schuster Speakers Bureau at 1-866-248-3049 or visit our website at www.simonspeakers.com.

Book designed by Nina Simoneaux

The text of this book was set in Garamond.

Manufactured in the United States of America 0819 OFF

2 4 6 8 10 9 7 5 3 1

The Library of Congress has cataloged the hardcover edition as follows:

Names: Cherry, Alison, author.

Title: Ella unleashed / Alison Cherry.

Description: New York : Aladdin, 2018. | Summary: "Twelve-year-old Ella juggles her desire to become a dog show champion and her secret mission to find a girlfriend for her single father, only to learn neither dog nor dad readily bends to her will"— Provided by publisher.

Identifiers: LCCN 2018006333 |

ISBN 9781534412125 (hardcover) | ISBN 9781534412149 (eBook) |

Subjects: | CYAC: Fathers and daughters—Fiction. | Single-parent families— Fiction. | Divorce—Fiction. | Dogs—Fiction. | Dog shows—Fiction. | Dating services—Fiction. | Science—Methodology—Fiction. |

BISAC: JUVENILE FICTION / Animals / Dogs. | JUVENILE FICTION / Family / Marriage & Divorce. | JUVENILE FICTION / Social Issues / Friendship.

Classification: LCC PZ7.C41987 Ell 2018 | DDC [Fic]—dc23

LC record available at https://lccn.loc.gov/2018006333

ISBN 9781534412132 (paperback)

FOR GEORGE HARRISON

— 1 —

My stepdad, Krishnan, claims dogs can't literally smell fear. But I'm pretty sure he's wrong, because Elvis definitely knows how I'm feeling right now. When Krishnan's holding his leash, Elvis always seems perfectly calm, tail wagging and tongue out in a relaxed, happy pant. Now that I'm in charge, he won't stop straining against his collar, making a high-pitched whining sound, and trying to sniff the butt of every single dog we pass. And since there are eight hundred dogs in this convention center, that means a *lot* of sniffing.

I plant my feet and lift my chin like I'm at the barre in ballet class—if I try to project confidence and calm, maybe it'll rub off on him. I'm pretty sure I *look* put together, at least on the outside. I'm in my new purple dress with two giant pockets on the front, perfect for holding Elvis's treats. My hair is slicked back in a neat bun so it won't get in my face and distract me. I'm even wearing the lucky watermelon lip gloss my best friends and I always smear on before our big tests and competitions and performances.

I am the alpha dog, I think, but Elvis isn't buying it. He jumps up on me, both paws planted on my stomach, and when I push him down, he lunges for a fluffy standard poodle. Her handler hurries her away and shoots me a look full of daggers, and I call, "Sorry!" But honestly, I can hardly blame Elvis for that one. I want to touch the ridiculous pom-poms on the poodle's butt too.

"C'mon, silly boy," I tell him. "You need a good brushing before showtime." Mom and Krishnan have already bathed and blow-dried and trimmed him for today's show, and even after running around the parking lot to work off some extra energy, he looks pretty great. But this will be my very first time taking him into the ring myself, so he needs to look *perfect.*

Our grooming station is set up to the left of the giant purple banner that says CITY OF AMESBURY CHAMPIONSHIP DOG SHOW. I tug Elvis up the aisle, which is crowded with dogs and their people and lined with vendor booths. We pass Punk Pups, where a woman is selling tiny skull-printed bandanas and motorcycle helmets for dogs. Next to my favorite smoothie vendor, Stan's Smoothie Shack, is SoulPaws, which will take a cast of your dog's paw print and make it into a silver pendant you can wear. There are snacks made of organic meat and carob, fake ducks to help retrievers practice for hunting season, and dog jackets that cost more than my down parka. There's even a booth called Pooch Royale that sells legit dog *thrones* covered in velvet and pink ruffles.

My dad loves dogs and would think all this stuff is hilarious, and a pang goes through me when I remember that he'll probably never see it in person. Getting him into the same room as Mom's new husband is pretty much impossible; sometimes he even looks uncomfortable dropping me off in their driveway. He called this morning to wish me luck in the ring, and he'll listen to every detail tonight over dinner. I know that's probably the best he can do right now; it's not his fault that the divorce has been hard on him. But hearing a replay isn't the same as cheering me on in person, and even though it might be selfish to want my stepdad *and* my real dad to come watch me compete, I can't help wishing for it anyway.

I snap a photo of the closest throne and text it to Dad.

Me: Totally buying you this for your birthday.

When he doesn't respond right away, I send it to my best friends, Miriam, Jordan, and Keiko, and the "someone's typing" dots pop up right away.

Jordan: Perfect for pretty pretty princess Elvis! ♛
Keiko: Do they make those in human sizes?
Mir: Amaaaaaazing. Good luck today. You're gonna do awesome.

I never actually told Mir how nervous I am, but she always knows the right thing to say. I text back that I wish they were here, and all three of them respond with dog emojis and hearts.

"Good gravy, aren't those dog thrones *adorable?*" coos an older woman in a beagle-printed tracksuit as I pull Elvis away from the vomit-inducing ruffles. "This would be just *perfect* for our holiday cards, don't you think, Earl? We could put an itty-bitty tiara on Baby and get her a little fur-trimmed cape. . . ."

Mom and Krishnan grin and wave when they see me approaching; I think my stepdad is even more excited than I am that I'm competing for the first time today. When my mom started dating him two years ago and told me he was a dog show guy, I was a little worried—I thought his house would be covered in massive oil paintings of dogs playing poker and "Love Me, Love My Dog" throw pillows. But he turned out to be a totally regular guy who happened to love Welsh springer spaniels, and after he took me to the Westminster Kennel Club dog show in New York City last year, I got hooked too. When I decided I wanted to try handling, Krishnan spent countless hours practicing with Elvis and me in the backyard. I want to be absolutely flawless today so he'll feel like all the time he spent was worth it.

"Hey, Ella," he calls when we get close. "How'd things go outside?" Elvis leaps with joy at the sight of his beloved owner, and his tail goes completely insane when my stepdad rubs his long auburn ears.

"Good," I say. "I managed to keep him from rolling in anything."

"Did he pee?"

"Yeah." Talking about Elvis's bathroom habits used to really embarrass me, but now I can discuss dog pee with the best of them. It makes me proud, in a weird way.

"Perfect," Krishnan says. "Let's give him one last primp."

My mom and stepdad swing their forty-five-pound dog onto the grooming table in one smooth motion—they go to shows practically every weekend, so they've had tons of practice—and Mom hands me a brush. When I glance over at the table to my left, I spot a tiny woman rubbing powdered chalk all over her enormous sheepdog to make him look whiter, which is totally against the rules. On our other side, a woman in a sweatshirt that says MY DOG IS PAWESOME is sneakily darkening the white spots on her bulldog's muzzle with an eyeliner pencil.

"You feeling ready?" Mom asks as I make sure Elvis's belly fur is perfectly straight.

My stomach jumps at the thought of a judge's sharp eyes on me. When Krishnan took Elvis into the ring to compete against all the other Welsh springer spaniels earlier today, the judge was just looking for the most perfect dog. Later today, the dog who won—the Best of Breed—will move on to compete against the winners of the other twenty-five breeds in the sporting group. Then the best sporting dog will go up against the winners of the six other groups: herding dogs, working dogs, terriers, hounds, toys, and non-sporting dogs. The very best dog of all will be named Best in Show.

In junior showmanship, though, there's only one single shot to impress the judge, who ranks the *kids* on how well we handle our dogs. I'm the one who has to be perfect, not Elvis.

But I say, "Yeah, I'm ready. We did great when we practiced yesterday, didn't we, Elvis?" I've been over each movement in my head a million times this morning, and I'm sure I've got them down.

"You guys are going to do so well today," Mom says. She glances at her phone. "It's almost time—we should get going."

I give Elvis a once-over; he looks soft and shiny from his nose to the tip of his swishy tail. "All right. Let's go, buddy," I say. "We're gonna kick some doggy butt." For just one second, I allow myself to imagine winning my very first time in the ring. I would get a million likes on Instagram if I posted a selfie with my dog and my ribbon, and my parents would be so ridiculously proud.

I check my phone, but Dad still hasn't texted back. I shove it into my pocket and try not to think about it.

On the way to my ring, we pass a group of bichons competing for Best of Breed; they look like a bunch of giant cotton balls bouncing in a circle. We skirt around two women who have their dogs' faces bedazzled on the backs of their jackets, and then we're at ring ten, where a few juniors are already lined up. I check in with the steward and collect Elvis's show number, which Krishnan rubber bands to my upper arm, and he and Mom hug me and wish me luck. Then they settle into empty plastic chairs across the ring, and I get in line behind few other girls and one boy.

A wave of nerves washes over me the second I'm on my own, and my clenched hand begins to sweat around the fancy beaded show leash. Elvis senses my change of mood and immediately starts getting antsy again, pulling me forward so he can sniff the butt of the German shepherd in front of us.

I tug him back. "*No!* Stay. I'm the alpha dog, not you."

"First time?" asks a girl from behind me.

She looks a couple years older than me—maybe a freshman in high school—and like almost everyone here, she's wearing a matching jacket and skirt with sparkles around the cuffs, collar, and hem. Should I have gone for an outfit like that? What is it with dog shows and sequins?

"Just psyching myself up," I say. The girl raises one eyebrow, and I sigh. "Okay, yes. I mean, for me it is—not for him. Is it that obvious?"

"You're going to do fine," she says, which isn't exactly an answer, but her friendly smile makes me feel a little calmer. "What's your dog's name?"

That seems like it should be an easy question. But I'm not sure if she means his everyday name or his long, complicated show name—Champion Chernushka's Lucky Number Seven—which includes his rank, the name of the kennel where he was born, and something related to his mom's name, Viva Las Vegas. I don't think I can get the show name out without feeling ridiculous, so I say "Elvis" and hope for the best.

The girl nods, so I guess I got it right. "He's beautiful," she says.

"Thanks. What's yours named?"

"This is Dempsey." Her dog has dreadlocks that reach all the way to the floor, kind of like a living mop.

"Those dogs are so funny-looking," I say. "In a good way, I mean. Does he take forever to dry when you give him a bath?"

"Almost an entire day. And you wouldn't believe how bad he smells when he's wet." She wrinkles her nose. "I'm Amber, by the way."

I smile when I realize we swapped our dogs' names but forgot to exchange our own—that makes me an official dog person, I think. Krishnan and I know all the dogs at the neighborhood park, but we refer to all the humans as "Hazel's owner" or "Pretzel's dad."

"I'm Ella," I say. Dempsey starts tugging on his leash, and Amber reaches into her bra and pulls out a treat for him. It seems like that would be an uncomfortable place to store them; I bet she wishes her skirt had pockets like mine does. Then again, it's way better than carrying your dog's treats in your own mouth, which I've seen tons of people do. I mean, I love Elvis and everything, but that is *vile*.

"So, have you competed in lots of shows before?" I ask Amber.

"Maybe five or six," she says like it's no big deal. "I'm trying to get my third win so I can qualify for the National Dog Show in Philadelphia. Have you been? It's really fun."

"I'm actually competing there this year," I say. "I won one of the lottery spots." Just saying the words makes my stomach knot up. Getting randomly chosen from a pool of kids to compete in such a big important show seemed exciting and cool when I read the "You've been selected" e-mail in the safety of my mom's kitchen. But if I'm this nervous for a show with six other juniors, I have no idea how I'm going to manage competing against thirty.

"Oh, cool," says Amber, but she sounds slightly less friendly now. I guess that makes sense, since she deserves the spot way more than I do. But I'm planning to compete in at least two or three more shows before the National Dog Show, so there's still time for me to rack up a few wins. If all goes well, I'll feel like I really earned it by the time I get there.

"All intermediate juniors in the novice class to the ring," calls the steward, and my heart kicks up another notch.

"Good luck," says Amber.

"Thanks, I need it," I say. "Good luck to you too."

The kids in front of me file into the ring, and I take a deep breath and get ready to follow. Mom and Krishnan beam at me, and I try to smile back. *You've got this*, I tell myself. *You were terrified before your solo in the spring dance recital, and it went perfectly. You know exactly what to do.*

Then again, my dad was there in the very front row of that dance recital, making our secret "good luck" hand signal: two thumbs-ups with the thumbs crossed to make an X. It's always so much easier to compete and perform when all the people I love are there to cheer me on. But having divorced parents means making compromises, and not having Dad here today is just another thing I'm going to have to deal with.

I draw myself up to my full five feet and hold my head high. "Come on, boy," I say to Elvis. "Time to go."

He looks up at me with his big liquid eyes, and then he sits down.

"Elvis!" I say. "Come! Come on!" I tug on his leash, but he just stares up at me, tongue hanging out and tail wagging. It's not the same wag he did for Krishnan earlier; this one is more of a slow *thump-thump-thump* against the floor. He's clearly trying to tell me something, but I don't speak tail wag.

"Do you want a treat?" I ask. His tail speeds up when he hears that word, so I pull one out of my dress pocket and hold it up to lure him into the ring. He focuses on it for a second . . . and then everything goes wrong at once.

Elvis launches himself at me and clamps his jaws around my skirt like a furry shark snacking on a seal. The world suddenly feels like it's moving in slow motion, and I have time to feel my pocket ripping off, to see the treats scatter across the carpet, to hear the gasps of the crowd around the ring. I have time to think about what an unbelievably stupid rookie mistake it was to carry my dog's treats *right at his nose level*—no wonder Amber keeps hers in her bra. And then a cool breeze kisses my thighs, and I watch the steward's mouth form a perfect O, and I realize it's not only my pocket that's gone. The entire front panel of my dress is torn up to the waistband, exposing my Wonder Woman underwear to the whole convention center.

I frantically gather the fabric around my legs, all my hopes of a perfect first show evaporating in a puff of smoke. There won't be a beautiful purple ribbon or a triumphant Instagram post. There's only me and my burning-red cheeks and my ripped dress and my dog, who's zooming around the floor and inhaling treats like this is the best day of his life.

I manage to plaster on a fake smile and tell Amber to go around me. But the moment she's gone, my eyes well up, and a huge lump makes itself at home in my throat. I've been training for this for six months, and now I can't even go into the ring, and it's all my fault. When I was shopping for show dresses, I only considered which pockets would be most convenient for *me*. I never even considered that they'd be equally convenient for Elvis. How could I have forgotten such an important variable?

I did *almost* everything right. But "almost" doesn't count in competition. "Almost" is the difference between being a champion and a laughingstock.

— *2* —

Mom is out of her seat in seconds, and before I know it she's beside me, bundling me into her long trench coat. Krishnan makes his way toward me more slowly, and the minute he arrives, Elvis trots right over to him, calmly wagging his tail. It's like he's a different dog now that I'm out of the equation.

Mom wraps an arm around my shoulders and leads me away from the ring. I glance back at the judge, desperately hoping she didn't see what happened—the same judges go to a lot of the shows, so it's possible I could come face-to-face with her in another ring someday. But she's inspecting the beagle that was first in line, not paying any attention to me at all. At least *one* thing has worked out today.

"You okay, Ellabella?" Mom asks.

I shrug and look at the floor. "I guess."

"I'm so sorry about what just happened, but we're still really proud of you. It took guts to get up there and try something new, and I think you're so brave, even if it didn't go quite as planned."

Didn't go quite as planned is the understatement of the century. "I should've known what was going to happen if I carried those treats in my pocket," I say. "How did I miss that?"

"Hindsight is twenty-twenty," Krishnan says. "Seriously, don't beat yourself up about it. Nobody's perfect on the first try."

"Yeah," I say. "But there's 'not perfect,' and then there's today." It's not like I *always* get things right on the first try—I have to practice to get good at stuff, like everyone else. But even though it seems braggy to say so, I usually pick things up pretty fast. It's always been easy for me to get good grades, I'm learning my Torah portion for my bat mitzvah way faster than Miriam, and I'm nailing my choreography for the winter dance recital. When I do mess things up, it's never for reasons as stupid as *this*.

"Trust me, I've seen worse," says Krishnan. "At a show last spring, I saw a fox terrier bite a Norwich terrier, and the owners got into a fistfight right in the ring."

"There was blood everywhere," Mom says. "Dog *and* human. It was really gross."

"And during a show last year, a Clumber spaniel swallowed her handler's engagement ring, and she had a total meltdown," Krishnan continues. "She kept screaming, 'He ate the symbol of our love!'"

That makes me crack a smile. "You're making that up."

"I swear I'm not. Even if you train a dog really well, it's still a dog. Sometimes there's nothing you can do."

"Well, *I'm* not going to lose control again," I say. Mom and Krishnan exchange one of those looks that adults sometimes shoot each other when they think you're being melodramatic, but I don't care—I know exactly where I went wrong, and that means I can fix it. To prove it, I say, "I'm going to make a pouch for Elvis's treats that I can wear on my upper arm, where he won't be able to get them. Can you guys help me rig it up?"

"Sure," Krishnan says. "That's a great idea. We'll do it sometime next week."

"Can't we do it tonight? I could come back to your place for a little bit before I go to Dad's. Maybe Elvis and I could squeeze in some more practice so that—"

"Elvis is tired, sweetheart," my mom says. "He's had a long weekend. And your dad hasn't seen you since Friday morning."

I sigh. "Okay. But when's the next show with a junior division? I want to test the pouch out in the ring as soon as possible."

"There's a show in Hartford in two weeks," Krishnan says. "You're welcome to come with us, as always."

Mom pulls me closer and rubs my back. It's nice, and part of me wants to melt into her side and cling to her like a little kid. But I know the only thing that'll actually make me feel better is redeeming myself. I lead the way back to the grooming area, find some jeans, a T-shirt, and a hoodie in my dance bag, and head to the bathroom to change.

Mom and Krishnan have the grooming table and Elvis's beauty supplies all packed by the time I'm done, and an hour later, we're pulling up in front of my dad's house. I sleep here on Sundays, Mondays, and Wednesdays, and I'm with Mom and Krishnan a mile away on Tuesdays, Thursdays, and Saturdays. Fridays are up for grabs, depending on everyone's schedule. It can get annoying sometimes, but mostly I've gotten good at remembering which stuff to leave where. Dad's house is where we all lived before the divorce, and even though Mom seems way happier with Krishnan than she ever did with Dad, I always think how weird it must be for her to drop me off here when it's not her home anymore.

I grab my dog hair–covered backpack and dance bag out of the trunk and kiss Mom goodbye. "I love you so much, Ellabella," she says. "Call if you forgot anything, and have fun with your dad."

It's been two years since she moved out, but hearing her say "your dad" still sets off a little pang of discomfort deep in my center. My first clue that things weren't going to be okay between my parents was when Mom started saying that instead of "Dad," like she was trying to distance herself from us. But I just say, "Love you too. You guys will check and make *sure* there are no junior competitions next weekend, right?"

"I promise," Krishnan says. "I'm proud of you for getting right back on the horse."

"Of course," I say. As if a horse could possibly kill my spirit by throwing me off *once*.

I dig my keys out of my backpack and head inside, and when I call hello, Dad answers from the kitchen. "Come in here, kiddo! My hands are covered in garlic."

I'm not sure if that's true or if it's an excuse not to come to the door until Krishnan's car is gone. But when I get to the kitchen, there's a pot of spaghetti sauce simmering on the stove, and Dad really is sliding a tray of garlic bread into the oven. He's gotten super into traditions since Mom moved out, and Italian Food Sundays is one of them. It's a little weird—when our family was in one piece, he was super laid-back and didn't care what food we ate when. Dr. Obasanjo, the therapist my parents sent me to after the divorce, apparently told him that sticking to routines was really important for my mental health, but he seems to care about it way more than I ever did.

Dad rinses his hands and pulls me into a tight hug. "Hey, I missed you. I hate going two whole days without seeing my girl."

"I missed you too," I say. "How was your weekend? What'd you do?" I really hope he went out with a friend or something. When he and Mom were married, they were always hosting dinner parties and going to shows and art galleries and restaurants and stuff. Mom and Krishnan still do things like that, but now Dad basically just goes to work and hangs out at home the rest of the time, sitting around in his grungy ripped jeans and reading biographies of dead white guys.

Dad shrugs. "Eh, nothing interesting. Errands and chores mostly. Watched some TV. Found some new recipes to try this week."

My heart sinks. I hate that he's become this faded version of the dad he was before, like he's been washed too many times. I know I can't be here every second to keep his spirits up, but it sucks knowing how lonely and sad he must be on the days I'm with Mom.

"New recipes sound fun," I say, trying to keep my voice cheerful.

Dad opens the oregano and sprinkles an amount that seems completely random into the spaghetti sauce. I don't understand how it's possible to cook without measuring anything. How can you be sure the food will turn out the way you expect when you don't follow a standardized procedure? "Yeah, some of them sound really tasty. By the way, I'm sorry I didn't respond to your text earlier. I was working in the yard. Those dog thrones were *horrifying*."

"I know, right?"

"Do people actually buy stuff like that?"

"I guess so," I say. "When I showed them to Krishnan, he said—"

Dad cuts me off before I can finish, even though he's the one who asked the question; I guess he doesn't actually want the answer if it involves my stepdad. "Tell me about the competition. How'd things go with Elvis?"

I wish I could let out all my frustration about today, but this is definitely the wrong place to do it. I try really hard to stay upbeat when I talk to Dad about my life; he already has enough on his mind, and I don't want to burden him with my problems on top of his own. Every time I mention that I'm unhappy about something, he seems so sad that he can't fix it for me that I feel guilty for bringing it up in the first place, and it's kind of a lose-lose situation. So instead of being honest, I decide to make the whole thing sound like a wacky comedy.

"Oh man, it was a disaster," I say, and then I give him a play-by-play in excruciating, slow-motion detail, complete with a demonstration that includes flailing my arms and rolling around on the kitchen floor. It's a total exaggeration, but I accomplish my mission of making Dad laugh. As long as he's still amused by my stupid antics, I'll know he's not feeling so down that I have to worry.

"Well, that doesn't sound like fun," he says when I'm back on my feet. "I'm sorry. No more dog shows for you, huh?"

I know he hates that I have a hobby in common with Krishnan, but it also sounds like he thinks I can't handle the challenge, and that stings. "No, I'm definitely trying again," I say, working hard to keep my voice level so it doesn't sound like I'm offended. "I have an idea for this pouch I'm going to make with Kr—um, that I'm going to make to carry Elvis's treats. By the time I get to the show in Philly, everything's going to be perfect."

"Well, okay. But if it would stress you out, it's perfectly fine to change your mind. I just want you to be happy."

"I'm not stressed," I say. "Maybe you could come to my next show and watch, though? It's in Hartford."

"Maybe," Dad says. But he can't meet my eyes, and I know that means no.

"But you'll come to Philly for the National Dog Show for sure, right?"

The timer goes off, and Dad grabs a pot holder and turns to pull the garlic bread out of the oven. "I don't know, Ellabee," he says. "Philly's kind of far, and I'm not sure what my schedule will be with work and stuff. We'll see."

Dad never works on the weekends, and Philadelphia's not *that* far from Boston. But I know this isn't about the distance or his schedule, and it makes an ache bloom in the center of my chest. Usually I'm able to keep the things I do with Dad and the things I do with Mom and Krishnan separate. But what's going to happen at my bat mitzvah in the spring? What's going to happen at my middle school graduation, or my high school graduation, or my college one? What if I get *married* someday? How can I have everyone I love there to support me at my big life events when Dad won't even stand near Krishnan for as long as it takes to run a dog around a ring?

Part of me wants to say all that out loud, but I know I shouldn't push Dad to do things that make him uncomfortable. So I swallow down the hurt, force my face into a neutral expression, and say, "Okay." I've got two whole months before the Philly show. Maybe I can work out a way to get him there by then.

The food is ready, and Dad serves us spaghetti and meatballs and garlic bread on the mismatched plates he got at a garage sale after Mom took half the dishes. He makes sure I get my favorite one with the blue octopus in the middle, which is especially perfect for eating spaghetti because of the way the tentacles and the noodles curl in the same way.

"Think up any good taglines this week?" I ask as we settle in at the kitchen table. Brainstorming with Dad always cheers me up. He's actually used variations on my ideas for real ads a few times.

He rolls his eyes. "We're *still* working on the Breezy detergent account. The client didn't like anything we came up with, so we have to start from scratch. I am so sick of this detergent."

"What about 'Easy, Breezy, lemon-squeezy'?"

"Not bad, but it's pretty similar to a tagline for a makeup company. Plus the product doesn't smell like lemons."

"What does it smell like?"

Dad thinks as he chews a meatball. "Like . . . a Christmas tree dunked in chemicals."

"Like those air fresheners in cars?"

"Almost exactly like that, yeah."

"Gross," I say. "Are people actually going to wash their clothes in that?"

Dad smiles. "They will if the advertising is good enough."

"Breezy: For when you need to cover up the smell of moldy

fast-food wrappers in your glove compartment," I say. It's not even that funny, but I'm tired and slaphappy enough that it sends me into a fit of hysterical giggles. A noodle falls out of my mouth, which just makes everything even more hilarious.

"Breezy," Dad says, handing me a bunch of napkins. "Your kid may be disgusting, but your clothes don't have to be."

When we're done, we curl up on the couch with bowls of Chunky Monkey ice cream and watch one of those nature shows where a super-calm British guy narrates as fish lay eggs and plants grow in fast motion. It comforts me to hear about how everything in nature happens according to predictable patterns. As soon as the show ends, I tell Dad I'm sleepy and head straight up to bed. It really has been a long day, but mostly I'm tired of hiding how annoyed and humiliated I am by my disaster in the ring. I want to wash this fake smile off my face and have a good long sulk under the covers.

Dad comes in to kiss me good night, and I paint the smile back on long enough for him to say, "Sweet dreams, Ellabee. I'm so glad you're here."

"Me too," I say.

He goes to my door and turns off the light, but then he pauses. "You seemed a little off while we were watching the polar bears. Do you want to talk about anything that happened today at the show?"

I shake my head. "No, I'm fine. I'm just tired."

"You sure?"

"Yup," I lie.

"All right. Well, see you in the morning."

"Good night," I say.

He finally closes the door, and I finally, *finally* lie back on the pillows and let my face relax. I know I'm doing the right thing by protecting Dad's feelings, but it's exhausting, constantly trying to cheer him up and worrying about whether I'm going to say the wrong thing. I'd be a lot more okay if only I could be certain that *he* is.

— 3 —

I can't wait to get to school the next morning so I can talk to my friends about the dog show. Luckily we all have fourth-period science with my favorite teacher, Ms. McKinnon. Miriam, Keiko, Jordan, and I plunk our stuff down on our favorite lab table, and I talk as fast as possible so I can cram in everything I want to say before the bell rings. They already know the basics of what happened, of course—I texted with them for most of the drive home last night. But the thing about best friends is that nothing feels real until you've hashed it out in person. This time I don't leave anything out, and my friends gasp and groan in all the right places. Nobody tries to convince me it wasn't as bad as I think, which makes me feel better, weirdly enough.

"Man," Jordan says. "Elvis seems like such a sweetie. I can't believe he did that to you."

"It was my fault," I say. "I should've thought things through better." A prickle of shame crawls over my skin, making me all hot and itchy.

"I'm sure it wasn't *totally* your fault," Keiko says. "Dogs are nuts. Once my aunt turned her back on her dog for one minute, and the dog swallowed two entire ears of corn, including the cobs. She had to have surgery to get them out."

"Oh god," Miriam says. "You guys are making me really happy I have fish."

"At least no one posted any photos or videos of me in my underwear," I say. "I've checked, like, fifty times."

The bell rings, and Ms. McKinnon comes out of the supply closet in the back of the lab carrying a big metal cylinder. She has on her Converse sneakers with the sparkly rainbow stars, and when she sets down the container, I see that the T-shirt under her lab coat is printed with sharks flying through space. I wish I could steal all her clothes.

"Take your seats, scientists!" she calls. "I've got a surprise for you."

Everyone sits down and shuts up right away. In most classes, a "surprise" means something like watching a boring video about the American Revolution instead of listening to a boring lecture about the American Revolution. But Ms. McKinnon's surprises are super weird and interesting—I did a two-week intensive science camp with her this past summer, and she was always lying on beds of nails and making stuff explode and bringing in weird animals.

"Madigan, on Friday you asked what would happen if you froze a Gummi bear with liquid nitrogen and hit it with a hammer. You still interested in finding out?" Madigan nods eagerly, and Ms. McKinnon says, "Good, because I thought we'd start off today by giving it a try." She reaches into her desk drawer and pulls out a big bag of Gummi bears, and everyone squeals and murmurs with excitement.

"Split into groups of four. Each group needs a beaker, a pair of forceps, and a hammer, and *everyone* needs safety goggles and gloves—liquid nitrogen can give you frostbite if it touches your bare skin. When you're finished gathering your materials, write a hypothesis for what you think will happen to a frozen Gummi bear and a room-temperature Gummi bear when they're hit with a hammer, and then we'll get to it."

My friends and I collect our supplies, write our hypothesis, and then return to the more important topic at hand. "So did your dad freak out when Elvis attacked you?" asks Miriam. "You said he didn't seem super happy that you were doing dog shows."

"He actually wasn't there," I say.

Mir's eyebrows scrunch together. "Because of your stepdad?"

I nod. "But it was your first show ever! I can't believe he didn't go."

"He's going to the big show in November, though, right?" Keiko asks. "*We're* all going."

I shrug. "He said 'We'll see,' but I know that means he won't."

"Even if you tell him how important it is?" Mir asks.

"I don't know if I should. Every time I talk about something related to Krishnan, he shuts the conversation down. It doesn't seem right to push him too hard."

"He needs to get over himself," Jordan says. "He's supposed to be the grown-up."

Ms. McKinnon comes over to our table to drop off our test

Gummis . . . and a whole handful more for us to eat. "Save two of the same color for the experiment," she says. "We don't want any variables besides how frozen they are." I love how exact she's being about this just-for-fun experiment. Science is so great that way—when you keep all the variables under control, you can almost always make an experiment turn out the way you want. And if something doesn't work, you figure out the step where you went wrong, change it, and try again until it does. Nothing is ever random.

My friends and I all like the orange Gummis least, so we set a couple of them aside and dig in to the rest of our pile. Ms. McKinnon grabs the container of liquid nitrogen and moves toward Madigan's table—her group gets to go first since the experiment was her idea.

"What if you got your dad to bring a date to the Philly show?" asks Keiko. "Then maybe he wouldn't care as much if Krishnan were there with your mom."

The idea is so ridiculous that I actually snort. "My dad doesn't go on *dates.*"

"Maybe he should," Keiko says.

"We could set him up with someone," suggests Jordan.

I try to imagine my dad choosing to put on nice clothes and sit in a restaurant with some random woman instead of watching baseball at home in his comfy chair, and I totally can't see it. Then again, if movies are anything to go by, falling in love makes sane adults run around in the rain and climb on kids' playground equipment and smear cupcake frosting on each other's noses. If it can do *that*, surely it can help turn someone back into his old self . . . the kind of person who might come watch his kid compete in a dog show.

Actually, the more I think about it, the more I realize that finding Dad a girlfriend is just good science. When he was with Mom, he was so much more easygoing and spontaneous and motivated. He came to all my recitals and performances and competitions, and I never had to protect his feelings or watch what I said around him. If I can bring the love variable back up to its original level, he won't be lonely or upset anymore, and everything else will go back to normal too. I can't believe I didn't think of it myself.

"Huh," I say. "Maybe we *should* set him up with someone."

There's a loud whacking sound from Madigan's table, and everyone cheers. I know her lab group is just excited about the experiment, but it feels like a vote of confidence.

Mir pops a Gummi into her mouth and chews carefully to avoid getting it stuck in her braces. "So, who do we know who's not married?"

"There must be a bunch of people in our class with divorced parents." Jordan looks around the room. "I think Ethan Fenton's parents got divorced last year. And his mom is the one who made those amazing brownies for the band bake sale."

I glance over at Ethan, who has a Gummi bear sticking out of each nostril. "A million brownies wouldn't make up for having *him* as a stepbrother," I say. "Don't you guys have any single relatives? Then I could be related to you."

"My great-aunt Rivka is single, but she's, like, eighty," Miriam says.

"I don't have anyone but my aunt Libby," says Jordan, "and she's the *worst.*"

"Really? We hadn't heard," Keiko says, and Jordan throws a red

Gummi at her. Her aunt moved to town at the beginning of the summer, and Jordan spends a *lot* of time complaining about her.

"Okay, what about our teachers?" Keiko asks. "What about Ms. Lapata?"

"Ms. Lapata's mean," I say. "She's always yelling at me."

"She wouldn't do that if you actually brought your PE uniform to school ever," Miriam says.

"I'm not setting my dad up with our gym teacher. She'd probably make me run laps if I didn't make my bed."

Ms. McKinnon walks up with her cylinder of liquid nitrogen. She's wearing her safety goggles on top of her regular glasses, which makes her eyes look hilariously gigantic. "You ready, girls?" she asks. "Safety goggles and gloves on. What's your hypothesis?"

I pull my goggles down over my eyes and settle them into place, and even though I know I look dorky, it makes me feel professional and scientific. "We think the unfrozen Gummi will spring back to its original shape right away when we hit it with the hammer and the frozen one will break into at least four pieces."

"All right, good theories. Let's test. Give the control Gummi a beating."

Jordan grabs the hammer and pounds on one of the orange test Gummis—she does martial arts, so she's super strong. It gets stuck to the head of the hammer, but nothing else interesting happens.

"Good. Now let's add the nitrogen." Ms. McKinnon opens her container and carefully pours some clear liquid into our beaker. It immediately begins to boil and steam, and all four of us go, *"Whoa."*

"Liquid nitrogen boils at −195.8 degrees Celsius," Ms. McKinnon says. "So even if we did this outside on the coldest day of the year, it would still boil. Amazing, huh? You can use your forceps to drop the Gummi in now."

Keiko does, and then we wait for the liquid nitrogen to boil off. "All right," Ms. McKinnon says after about fifteen seconds. "Go ahead and grab it, and let's see what happens."

Miriam gingerly pulls the bear out with the forceps and lays it on the lab table. It looks frosty and fragile. "You want to do the honors?" she asks me.

"Definitely." I take the hammer and give the frozen bear a good whack, and it splinters like the brittlest glass. Tiny pieces of orange sugar fly everywhere, and we all squeal.

Ms. McKinnon laughs. "Cool, right?"

"So cool!" I say.

"Grab some paper towels and wipe up the pieces before they melt into a huge mess, and then record your findings in your lab notebooks. Good job, girls."

As I watch our teacher walk toward the next group, a light bulb goes off in my brain. "Oh my god," I whisper to my friends. "We should set my dad up with *her*."

Miriam's eyes widen. "She would be *perfect*! I bet they'd like each other so much!"

"Oh man, she'd be the best stepmom," Keiko says. "She'd probably make chocolate-chip pancakes for dinner and wake you up in the middle of the night so you could watch meteor showers even if there was school the next day."

"I bet she'd never make you clean your room," says Jordan. "If you left moldy dishes under your bed, she'd get out her microscope and look at the spores with you."

"Are you sure she's single?" asks Miriam. "I can't remember if she wears a ring or not."

We glance over at Ethan's lab group as Ahmed brings his hammer down, and I pay special attention to our teacher's hands. She still has her gloves on, but she's holding the metal cylinder pretty tightly, and I don't see the outline of a ring.

"I think we're good," I say.

Keiko goes to the sink to get some paper towels and starts wiping up the smashed Gummi pieces, which are starting to melt. "So how are you going to introduce her to your dad?" she asks.

"You should do something really bad in class," Jordan suggests. "Then the school will call your parents in for a disciplinary meeting."

"Bad like what?" asks Miriam.

"I dunno. Kevin got suspended last year when he put that firecracker in the toilet."

I roll my eyes. "I'm not blowing up a toilet to get my dad a date!"

"Hang on," Miriam says. "Isn't that fall open house thing on Wednesday?"

"Oh my god, *yes*." I'm so excited I almost fall off my lab stool. "That's *perfect*. My dad always goes by himself because my mom has to run the one for her class on the same night."

"You're going to have to be there to help things along, though," Keiko says. "Your dad and Ms. McKinnon aren't going to randomly fall in love while they're talking about the science curriculum. Are we even allowed at the open house?"

"Probably not inside the classrooms, but there's a sign-up sheet outside the office to be a student volunteer and give directions. That way I can make sure they talk. You guys can sign up too!"

"I have trumpet on Wednesdays," Keiko says at the same time as Jordan says, "I have tae kwon do."

"I promised my mom I'd watch my brother," Miriam says. "Do you want me to try to get out of it?"

"No, it's fine. I can handle it by myself." Having my friends with me would definitely make the open house more fun, but maybe it's better that they won't be there to distract me. I'll need to concentrate and make sure everything is perfect. "You guys," I say. "This is going to be *epic.*"

"I bet that in the entire history of the world, nobody's ever said that about the fall open house," says Jordan.

Miriam pulls out her lab notebook and starts recording the results of our experiment, and the rest of us do the same. But even as I'm writing about frozen Gummi bears, my mind is far away, spinning an amazing love story that's going to fix everything.

— 4 —

I know the hallways of Florence Nightingale Middle School like I know my own reflection, but even so, being at school after-hours always seems mysterious and exciting. I ride my bike over early so I can sign up to be stationed in the science hallway, and Ms. McKinnon's classroom is still dark when I plant myself outside her door. I'm glad I was able to talk Dad out of driving me here; I'm so nervous and excited that I probably would've babbled and giggled the entire time and given away that I was plotting something.

Ms. McKinnon arrives twenty minutes before the open house is supposed to start. She's in a simple black dress, which is kind of disappointing—I was hoping she'd wear one of her funny T-shirts so my dad could see what a good sense of humor she has. But she looks really pretty, and she has on a huge necklace made of gears and chains and watch faces, which I think Dad will really like. Plus her glasses are almost the same exact shade of turquoise that's in the plaid shirt I suggested he wear. I don't know if people are more likely to fall for each other if they're wearing matching clothes, but it can't hurt.

Ms. McKinnon smiles when she sees me standing by her door. "Hey, Ella," she says. "Thanks so much for helping out tonight."

"Yes," I say, and it comes out a little breathless. "I mean, you're welcome, no problem, I'm happy to be here." She looks at me weird, so I change the subject to distract her from the fact that I'm acting like a total freak show. "So, um, are you nervous about the open house?"

She laughs. "Not really. Should I be? Are your parents scary?"

I shake my head so hard my ponytail almost whips me in the eyes. "No! Definitely not. My mom actually isn't coming because she's a teacher too, so she's having her own open house tonight. Plus my parents are *divorced*"—I draw the word out nice and slow so she's sure to take it in—"so they don't go to stuff together. But I'm really, really excited for you to meet my dad. He's so nice, and I told him all about you, so he already thinks you're awesome. He said that if his teachers had let him do stuff like smashing frozen Gummi bears, maybe he would've become a scientist instead of an advertiser." Okay, so maybe that's not *exactly* what he said, but I'm pretty sure he was thinking it.

"Well, I look forward to meeting him," Ms. McKinnon says. "I'm going to go get ready. Let me know if you need anything, okay?"

I really want to say, *I need you to take my dad on a date so he'll fall in love with you and live happily ever after and also agree to come to a dog show in Philadelphia,* but obviously I can't. So I just say, "Okay, thanks."

I have some time to kill, so I review the notes I typed into my phone yesterday during a marathon of *Heart2Heart*, a dating show where people compete to see how many of their friends they can successfully set up in one week. I learned that the best way to get people to like one another is to tell stories that make them seem really interesting and funny, then introduce topics they have in common so they'll have lots of things to talk about. Of course, my dad and Ms. McKinnon already have something to talk about—the science curriculum—but I have a feeling that's not going to make them feel very romantic. I'll have to nudge them in the right direction.

Parents start arriving and trickling into Ms. McKinnon's classroom, but my dad is nowhere to be found—I guess he started out with the language arts and social studies classrooms on the floor below us. Half an hour later, when I'm starting to get really impatient, he finally appears, casually strolling down the hall like his life isn't about to change. I give him a big smile.

"Hey, kiddo," he says. "Seems like you have some really great teachers this year. Ms. Baumgartner says—"

"That's awesome," I say before Dad can even tell me *what* exactly is awesome. "Come in here, I really want you to meet Ms. McKinnon." The volunteers aren't technically supposed to go inside the classrooms, but nobody stops me as I take him by the arm and tug him inside. Sometimes it's just a matter of looking confident.

Ms. McKinnon is leaning on her desk, chatting with five or six parents grouped around her like kids at story hour. I watch my dad's face as he sees my teacher for the first time—Keiko told me people's pupils dilate when they look at someone they find attractive—but the fluorescent classroom lights make it hard to tell if anything is happening.

"Hi, are you—" Ms. McKinnon calls out, and then she breaks into a smile. "Oh wow, I don't even need to ask. You *must* be Mr. Cohen. You and Ella have the same exact eyes and nose."

"Same exact hair, too," my dad says. He fluffs the stubbly fringe around his bald head, and Ms. McKinnon laughs, which seems like a good sign. People make jokes when they're flirting, right?

I laugh too, but it comes out loud and manic, like the time I downed four Cokes at Miriam's birthday party. All the other parents look at me weird, but I ignore them. "You're so funny," I say to my dad. "Isn't he *too funny*?"

Ms. McKinnon sticks out her hand, and my dad goes over to shake it. "I'm Candice McKinnon, and I teach seventh- and eighth-grade science," she says.

"David Cohen," my dad says. I'm hoping he'll hold onto her hand a beat too long, like Stacey and Vince on *Heart2Heart* did right before they fell in love, but it looks like a pretty regular handshake. "It's nice to meet you. Ella speaks really highly of you."

"I think she's pretty great too," Ms. McKinnon says. "Speaking of which: Ella, you're not really supposed to be in here."

"Yeah, okay," I say, but I can't possibly go back outside yet. I need some time to do wingman stuff. (Or would it be wingwoman? Wing-girl?) I pretend I'm going to move toward the door, but then I stop like I've just thought of something. "Hey, Dad—before she moved here, Ms. McKinnon taught at a school in Ohio. Isn't that a coincidence?"

"Oh, where in Ohio?" my dad asks her, like I hoped he would. "That's where I grew up."

"Akron," Ms. McKinnon says. "What about you?"

"Cincinnati."

"I grew up near Columbus," says a woman I'm pretty sure is Danny Spindler's mom.

"Very cool," says Ms. McKinnon, and then they all just stand there nodding, like that's all there is to say about the entire state of Ohio.

"Maybe you and Ms. McKinnon have been to some of the same restaurants or something," I say to my dad to move things along.

Dad laughs. "I don't think so. Cincinnati and Akron are pretty much on opposite sides of the state."

"But you must've gone to Akron when you toured with your band, right?" I'm pretty sure women are supposed to fall for guys in bands, and I search Ms. McKinnon's face for signs that she's impressed, but instead she looks half amused, half confused.

My dad's cheeks are turning red. "Wow, Ella," he says. "What on earth made you think of that?"

"What kind of band?" asks Mei-Ying Cho's dad. "I was in a band in college too. Kind of hipster-punk? We were called Tragedy Soup." Mei-Ying's mom pats his arm and gives him a look like *Nobody wants to hear this*, and I totally agree. This conversation is supposed to be about *my* dad.

Dad runs his hand over the bald part of his head like he always does when he's nervous or embarrassed. "Mine was barely a band. Just a bunch of guys abusing instruments. You know how it goes."

"He's being modest," I say. "He's really great at guitar. He only has to hear a song, like, two times, and he can play it with no mistakes." I turn back to my dad. "Tell Ms. McKinnon what _your_ band was called." My dad gives me a look that says _What are you doing?_ and it doesn't seem like he's going to help me out here, so I say, "They were called the Unexpected Houseguests. Isn't that funny?"

"Nice," says Mei-Ying's dad, but Ms. McKinnon doesn't laugh—actually, she seems a little weirded out. Maybe I'm overdoing it with the wingwomaning.

"So, when is the science fair this year?" Danny's mom asks, and Ms. McKinnon finally smiles a real smile, obviously relieved to have the conversation back on track.

"The actual fair isn't until the week before winter break, but the kids will start choosing projects in a few weeks," she says. "Since the seventh graders are focusing on—"

"Excuse me, where's Mr. Wu's room?" calls another mom from the doorway, and Ms. McKinnon glances over at me like she's trying to subtly remind me that I have another job besides standing around in her classroom and talking about bands. I don't think there's much more I can do here anyway if everyone's just going to discuss the science fair, so I lead the confused mom back outside and point her in the right direction.

I linger by the science room door, trying to catch bits of the conversation, but it's too loud in the hall to hear anything. I cross all my fingers and hope that Ms. McKinnon and Dad are figuring out how compatible they are, but that doesn't seem likely—they haven't done a single thing the _Heart2Heart_ hosts would call a "heartthrob move." If Daphne Langoria, the show's dating specialist, were here right now, she'd probably say something about being stuck in the friend zone.

Then again, Dad and Ms. McKinnon have only known each other a few minutes; the *Heart2Heart* couples get way longer than that, and they always meet in fun, casual settings. Now that they've been introduced, maybe I can engineer another more relaxed meeting. If I can figure out what Ms. McKinnon's doing this weekend, maybe I can get Dad to take me to the same place and we can "unexpectedly" run into her.

Mei-Ying's parents come out of the science room, and Tess Revenaugh's parents go in, and then my dad finally appears. "So?" I ask. "How was it? Do you like her?"

"She seems great," my dad says. "Sounds like you guys have some cool projects planned. I know you're excited about the science fair, and you must be thrilled about the chick incubator she's bringing in—I know how much you loved the one at the Museum of Science last year."

I nod. "Yeah, that's gonna be *so* great. I can't wait."

"She said she and her boyfriend are doing a test run at home right now to make sure they have all the kinks worked out. Sounds like . . ."

Dad keeps talking, but I'm not paying attention anymore. All I hear is the word "boyfriend" echoing through my head over and over as my beautiful plan crumbles around me like a block tower smashed by a toddler.

Of *course* Ms. McKinnon has a boyfriend. How could I have been so stupid? Why would she be interested in my dad or impressed by his college band when she's already with someone else? Her boyfriend probably has tons of beautiful, thick hair. He's probably still *in* a band. I shouldn't have jumped to the conclusion that she was single just because she doesn't wear a ring. You should never jump to *any* conclusion that's supported by only one piece of evidence.

Down goes the image of my dad watching me compete at the National Dog Show.

Down goes the possibility of him and Krishnan and Mom all sitting in a calm, happy row at my bat mitzvah and my eighth-grade graduation.

Down, down, down goes the light, floaty feeling that would come from being myself without worrying about Dad's fragile feelings.

"Hey, kiddo? You okay?" he asks. "You spaced out for a second."

"Yeah. I just have a headache."

"Do you want me to ask Ms. McKinnon if she has any Tylenol?"

I shake my head. "No, it's fine. It doesn't hurt that much." I force my mouth into a smile.

It doesn't seem like he believes me, but he says, "All right, if you're sure. I'm going to take a peek into the other classrooms. Which one is next?"

I point. "Mr. Wu's my art teacher—his room is the second one on the right."

"Thanks." Dad wraps his arm around my shoulders and gives me a quick squeeze. "I'll meet you out front when you're done, and if you're feeling up to it, we can get some ice cream. Sound good?"

"Yeah, definitely," I say, though *nothing* sounds good right now, not even ice cream.

I watch the fluorescent lights reflect off Dad's shiny head as he walks away, and once he's safely in Mr. Wu's room, I slump down onto the floor with my back to the lockers and my forehead against my knees. I know there must be other solutions—there's never only one way to solve any problem. But Ms. McKinnon would've been such a good companion for my dad, and I have no idea how I'm going to find someone else to set him up with. It's not like I know tons of single women his age. Can't something just be *easy* for once?

I pull out my phone and open the group text I have going with Miriam, Keiko, and Jordan.

Me: Ms. McKinnon has a bf.

Me: Need plan B asap.

Me: HELP.

— 5 —

I must look extra gloomy the next day, because the second
Miriam sees me in homeroom, she calls an EVGAP (Emergency
Video Games and Pedicures) meeting at her house after school. We
haven't had one of those since Keiko's guinea pig died at the end of
July, and the fact that my friends are taking my disappointment so
seriously makes me feel a little better even before we get to the video
games and nail polish.

Miriam's house is close to school, so we walk over as soon as the
bell rings, load up on cheddar popcorn and peanut butter pretzels and
Oreos, and park ourselves in front of the TV in the basement. Since
Miriam only has two controllers, we take turns playing Mario Kart and
painting our toenails, switching off whenever someone is ready for a
new coat of polish. We talk about absolutely nothing for a few games,
and by the time I'm done with the silver polka dots on my big toes,
I'm starting to feel less horrible. The combination of salt, sugar, nail
polish fumes, and the hypnotic way the road passes on the screen lulls

me into a comfortable laziness, and I lie back on the carpet and close my eyes. Life would be so much easier if I didn't even have parents and I could stay here with Mir and Jordan and Keiko forever.

Jordan wins a race, does a victory dance, and tosses her controller aside. "So," she says, "what are we going to do about Ella's dad?"

"I don't knowwww," I groan. I flop over onto my side, careful not to touch the carpet with my not-quite-dry toenails. "I can't think of anyone else to set him up with. Where do people even meet each other after they stop going to school?"

"Parties?" says Jordan. "Bars?"

"I can't exactly go to a *bar* with my dad."

"What about the internet?" says Keiko.

I sit up so quickly I get a head rush. I'd totally forgotten online dating was a thing. The internet would provide a much larger pool of potential women, and all of them would actually be *available*.

"Isn't online dating kind of gross and weird, though?" I ask. "Do normal people do it?"

Keiko shrugs. "I don't know. My sister tried it, and she said all the guys were creepy."

"Do you think the women are creepy too, or is it only the guys? Or maybe the whole thing is less creepy if you're old. Do old people do online dating?"

Keiko wrinkles her nose. "I saw this commercial where *super* old people were doing it. Like, my grandma's age. It was gross."

"How is that gross?" Miriam asks. "My grandma got remarried in her seventies. It was sweet. My step-grandpa is the best."

"My aunt Libby uses this site called Head Over Heels," Jordan says. "She talks about it constantly. But if the other women on there are like her, your dad definitely shouldn't sign up, because—"

"—*she's the worst*," we all chorus, and Jordan nods, obviously pleased.

"Why don't we look at the site and see if there's anyone good?" Miriam retrieves her hand-me-down laptop, and we all crowd around the screen while the site loads.

I was expecting something pink and horrible, but the home screen is dark blue with a swirl of lighter blue and silver in the corner. It's actually kind of classy. When Miriam clicks on the button that says Get Started, a box pops up in the middle of the screen.

Welcome to Head Over Heels!

I am a _____ _____ looking for _____.

Each blank is a drop-down menu where you're supposed to select your gender and sexual orientation, but the lists are *really* long and confusing. "What's demisexual?" asks Keiko, peering over my shoulder. "What does nonbinary mean?"

"What's two spirit?" asks Jordan.

"Maybe we can look at the women without filling out this part." Miriam clicks around some more, but it doesn't seem like there's any way into the site without making a profile.

I flop back onto the carpet again. "It doesn't matter anyway," I say. "My dad would never agree to sign up for this."

"I mean . . . he wouldn't have to *know* about it," Keiko says around a mouthful of Oreo. "We could make a profile for him and see what happens. If we don't find anyone good, we can take it down. And if we do . . ." She shrugs.

I consider it. On the one hand, it seems kind of wrong to put my dad on a dating site without asking. But on the other hand, I'd be doing him a huge favor. Having an awesome girlfriend could only improve his life, and this way he wouldn't have to do any of the stressful work of finding someone. Plus, if I'm the one going through the profiles, there's no chance he'll end up with someone I don't like.

"Okay," I say. "Let's do it. Give me the computer."

My friends whoop. Miriam hands over the laptop, and I select "I am a STRAIGHT MAN seeking WOMEN" from the drop-down menus. It gives us another list of questions, so I enter some basic stuff like my dad's age and zip code and what languages he speaks. But when it asks for a username, I hesitate.

"ItalianChef?" suggests Miriam. "That's probably taken. ItalianChefFTW?" She's had a million spaghetti dinners at my house and really loves my dad's food.

"That makes him sound like he's Italian, though," Keiko says. "And like he works as a chef."

"SexyBaldStud?" Jordan says, and all of us shriek with horrified laughter.

When we finally calm down, I say, "What about something like SuperDad? He likes superhero stuff, and it lets everyone know he has a kid right away."

"It's kind of sappy," Jordan says.

But Mir and Keiko think it's cute, so I type it in. It's taken, but when I add his initials to the end, the website accepts it. I make up a password, and then the site asks me to upload a picture. I use the one from Dad's company's website; his smile looks nice, and it was taken a few years ago when he had a little more hair.

There are still tons of profile questions to fill out, but I figure I can do the rest later. I click the submit button, and a heart-shaped firework explodes in the center of the screen. *WELCOME, SUPERDAD_DSC! Ready to find love?* says the message that pops up, and Jordan makes a gagging sound, but my own heart does a happy little flip.

I click yes . . . and then my eyes bug out as a list of women's profiles pops up. I expected there to be a bunch, since I entered a large age range, but there are literally *thousands* of people. Face after face flashes past as I scroll down, and I start to panic. How am I going to read all of these?

"Whoa," says Keiko. "What if the perfect girlfriend is way at the bottom and you never even get to her?"

"Maybe you should *start* at the bottom," Jordan says.

"But then what if she was at the top the whole time?"

"Read the top and bottom and skip the middle?"

"But what if—"

"Click on that one," Miriam says, pointing to a woman with red hair who's hugging a golden retriever in her profile picture.

I read her About Me section aloud. "I'm a compassionate, passionate woman seeking a partner in crime for romance, mischief, and adventure! Don't be fooled by my polished exterior; I love pampering myself with spa days and manicures, but I'm an outdoorsy girl at heart, and I'm not afraid to get dirty. I'm not much of a sports fan, but I don't mind cheering for your favorite team. I've got a career I adore and a gorgeous apartment big enough for two, and now it's time to fill that empty space in my home and my heart."

"Ew," Jordan says. "Who talks about their own polished exterior? Isn't that basically another way to say, 'Look how pretty I am'?"

"Why would she assume every guy likes sports?" Keiko says. "My dad *hates* sports."

"Plus she says her apartment is only big enough for two," Miriam says. "Pass."

We read through a bunch more profiles, and I make some notes about things I should include when I finish my dad's later—at least half the women say things like "I'm not religious, but I'm spiritual" and "I'm just as comfortable doing [some super casual thing] as I am doing [some super fancy thing.]" There's a cardiologist, a bartender, and a woman who keeps bees who look promising at first, but it takes almost no time to rule them all out. The woman with the bees says her ideal first date is a trip to her psychic, which makes Jordan laugh so hard Sprite comes out of her nose. The bartender has four cats, and my dad is allergic. The cardiologist doesn't want kids.

I push the laptop away, overwhelmed and discouraged already. "This is stupid. There's nobody good on here."

Miriam peers at the screen. "Hang on, what's this?"

There's a heart icon in the corner of the page that I hadn't noticed until now, but it's pulsing softly. When Mir clicks on it, a whole different list of profiles pops up, along with a banner across the top.

Congratulations, SuperDad_DSC!

14 people like your profile!

Click here to start messaging your favorites!

As we watch, the number changes to fifteen. Then sixteen. Then seventeen.

"Oh my god," Jordan says. "He's *so popular*. How do *we* get that popular?"

She's right. My middle-aged bald dad, who's had a fake, incomplete profile up for half an hour, already has *seventeen people* who want to go on dates with him? I never even get likes that fast when I post stuff on Instagram.

This could be great, though. If this many people are interested in him, maybe I don't need to read through the millions of profiles after all. I just need to fill in the rest of his information, watch the messages roll in, and pick the potential girlfriends I like best.

WELCOME, SUPERDAD_DSC!

MY PROFILE: [click here to edit]

GENDER: Male
AGE: 43
LOCATION: Arlington, MA
HEIGHT: 5'11"
BODY TYPE: Average
ETHNICITY: White
MARITAL STATUS: Divorced
EDUCATION: College degree
CAREER: Advertising

SMOKES: Never
CHILDREN: Has kid(s)
PETS: Likes dogs, fish. Allergic to cats.
LANGUAGES SPOKEN: English (fluent); Spanish (a little)
LOOKING FOR: Women who like men, 35–50, for long-term dating/committed relationship

ABOUT ME:

Even though I'm divorced, I still believe in the power of love and am totally ready to be part of a couple again! I may come off as a little shy at first, but I promise I'll be making you laugh in no time once I get to know you! When I'm not at work, I love to cook (Italian food is my specialty), play my guitar, and watch nature documentaries, movies, and baseball (GO SOX!). I'm not religious, but I'm spiritual. My twelve-year-old daughter is my favorite person in the entire world, so . . . not looking for people who don't like kids.

WHAT I DO FOR A LIVING:

Copywriter at an advertising company. You've probably seen my ads on billboards and the sides of buses and stuff. Remember that one for Granolatastic breakfast bars with the rabbits and the turtles? That was mine!

MY FRIENDS DESCRIBE ME AS:

Funny. Smart. Great at being a dad!

FAVORITE BOOKS, TV SHOWS, MOVIES, MUSIC:

Books: Historical biographies. If it's a million pages long and has a black-and-white picture of a dead dude on the front, I'm probably interested. I also read all the *Harry Potter* books to my daughter, and I pretended to think they were just okay, but secretly I really liked them. TV shows: *Planet Earth, Cosmos, Deadliest Catch, The West Wing*. Movies: *Star Wars*. Period. (Except the prequels, obviously!) Music: Oldies.

IF I HAD A SUPERPOWER, IT WOULD BE:

Teleportation. I could take my daughter to see the world for free and have her back in time for school the next day. And I could get all my pizza from actual Italy, not the place down the street with the gross crust.

MY IDEAL FIRST DATE IS:

A long walk through the Public Garden, maybe a swan boat if we're feeling cheesy, and cooking you dinner. Or going out somewhere fancy, if you want. I'm just as comfortable in a suit and tie as I am in my Kiss the Cook apron!

GET IN TOUCH IF . . .

. . . you're looking for someone who will give you tons of love and attention! Bonus points if you like pasta! And kids!

To: SuperDad_DSC
From: PennyForYrThoughts
Hey there, SuperDad,
I was excited to find your profile today; it's really refreshing to see a dad who's so focused on his daughter. My kids are the center of my world too, and I couldn't be with anyone who didn't understand that. I am also a huge Sox fan and love to cook, and I feel like we might enjoy each other's company. Take a look at my profile and see what you think, and I hope to hear from you soon!
All the best,
Penny

To: PennyForYrThoughts
From: SuperDad_DSC
Hi, Penny! It IS nice to find someone who feels the same way about their kids. How many do you have, and how old are they, and are they boys or girls? What's your favorite thing to cook? I make an awesome spaghetti Bolognese!
David

To: SuperDad_DSC
From: PennyForYrThoughts
I've got two boys and a girl—my sons are twelve and six, and my daughter is eight. I asked them what the best thing I cook is, and the older two put in votes for my lasagna. My youngest said

"dinosaur chicken nuggets," so I guess I'm pretty great at pre-heating the oven? :) Are you and your daughter doing anything fun this weekend?

P

To: PennyForYrThoughts
From: SuperDad_DSC

We might go to the zoo on Sunday! Want to come? You could bring your kids, and we could all have a group hang.

D

To: SuperDad_DSC
From: PennyForYrThoughts

That's pretty unconventional, but honestly it sounds nice! Every guy I've been out with so far has tried his best to avoid meeting my kids. I like that you're different. Meet you at the Tropical Forest Pavilion at noon.

— 6 —

I spend most of Saturday practicing with Elvis and Krishnan—
we're working on making our turns tighter—and perfecting the pouch
I made for carrying dog treats. It closes with a magnet so that it flips
open easily and latches by itself, and I think Ms. McKinnon would be
proud of my creative engineering. But it's hard to keep my mind on
my work when I'm counting down the hours until I finally get to set
eyes on the woman who will hopefully become Dad's new girlfriend.

Sunday finally comes, and Keiko's mom drives my friends and
me to the Franklin Park Zoo in the morning. The second she leaves
to do some shopping, the four of us head straight for the conces-
sion stand—what's the point of being unsupervised if you can't eat
cotton candy before lunch? I'm so excited about Penny that I barely
have an appetite, but somehow I still manage to down my fair share
of blue fluff.

"What do you think she'll be like?" I ask my friends for the millionth time as we watch the zebras. "Do you think her kids will be cool? You guys, I could finally have siblings!"

"Ugh," Keiko says. "It's not all it's cracked up to be."

"Yeah, but your sisters are so much older. I could be the *best* cool older sister to a six-year-old and an eight-year-old. They would totally love me. And her son is my age! Maybe if I had a brother, I'd actually understand boys."

"Is understanding boys even possible?" Jordan asks.

"I don't know. Maybe! We could find out!"

My phone alarm goes off, blasting the special ring tone I set for today—"Super-Epic Romance" by SneakyMouse—and I leap off the bench we're sitting on. It's 11:55, which means Penny should be herding her kids toward the Tropical Forest Pavilion right now to "meet up with my dad." It's go time.

"Everyone remember the plan?" I ask, and my friends roll their eyes. We've been over the plan so many times they could probably recite it backward in Spanish in their sleep. We wrap up the remains of our cotton candy, and then we head past the giraffes and the Outback Pavilion and turn down the path to the Tropical Forest.

When it comes into view, I suddenly start to feel jumpy. Five minutes ago I was totally confident about my plan, but now it feels like maybe we're doing something wrong, luring Penny here for a date that's not really going to happen. After I scope her out, I'm going to write her a really nice e-mail from "my dad," making a good excuse for "standing her up" and asking her to reschedule. But what if she gets upset or angry anyway? She seems like a cool person, and it doesn't feel quite right to mess with her like this.

"Ella?" Miriam says, and I realize I've walked all the way to the door without realizing it. The expression on my friend's face makes me think this might not be the first time she's said my name. "Are you ready?"

I take a deep breath. "What we're doing is okay, right? It's not too mean?"

"Of course not," Keiko says. "How is it mean? We're trying to land her an awesome new boyfriend. Your dad is the best."

"Yeah, but she thinks she's meeting him *today*. I'm sure she's all nervous and excited, and then she'll be disappointed when he doesn't show up."

"She'll probably meet him eventually, though," Mir says. "You just need to do a little research first and make sure she's good enough for him. You're only trying to protect him. And in the meantime Penny will have fun at the zoo with her kids. It's not like we told her to meet us at a garbage dump or a dentist's office or something."

It's true. The zoo is fun regardless of whether you have a date, and I'm sure Penny's a reasonable person who understands that plans change sometimes. When she meets my dad for real, she'll probably like him so much that she'll forget this ever happened.

"Okay. You're right." I dig the lucky watermelon lip gloss out of my pocket and we pass it around, and then I say, "Let's do this."

We push through the doors into the dim humidity of the Tropical Forest, ripe with the smells of fruit and leaves and animal pee. It kind of reminds me of the end of the day at a dog show, when the doggy bathrooms start to get a bit disgusting. I don't see anyone who looks like Penny right away, but the gorilla enclosure is a big glassed-in peninsula that juts into the middle of the space, so there are lots of places she and her kids could be. It's hard not to get distracted by the lemurs and the ocelot and the ridiculously weird capybara as we make our way down the path, but I force myself to keep my eyes on the humans.

Keiko nudges me and tips her head toward a family looking at the pygmy hippos. "Is that them?"

I turn around slowly, trying not to look obvious. The woman near the hippos has the right haircut and three kids, but it's not her. "Nope," I whisper. "Those kids are too young, and her hair is too dark."

A huge commotion starts up to our left—some little boy is making incredibly loud "Hoo-hoo-hoo-ha-ha-ha" noises and doing that stupid monkey thing where you scratch your head with one hand and your armpit with the other. (What even is that? I've never seen an actual monkey do that.) There's a gorilla a few feet away on the other side of the glass, and she stares at the kid with this superior expression, like she's thinking about how basic he is.

And then the boy's mom turns around and says, "Dylan, you've got to stop, honey. The animals don't like that," and my heart lurches into my throat. She's got sandy hair and a friendly-looking face, and on her other side is a girl who looks about eight. Every few seconds the woman glances around hopefully, like she's waiting for something great to happen. It's definitely her, and she gets a big point in the plus column for how excited she looks about meeting my dad. Her older son doesn't seem to be with them, which is disappointing.

I duck out of sight around the corner of the tamarin enclosure. "The kangaroos are out today," I say, which is the code phrase my friends and I decided meant *I see them!*

"Where?" Miriam says. "I mean, where do they keep the . . . kangaroos?"

"Around the other side of this wall," I say. "They're making a lot of noise right now."

Jordan's eyes go wide. "Oh no," she says. "Not *those* kangaroos."

I shush her, even though I agree that the annoying kid goes in the minus column. "Stick to the plan. It's not about the baby kangaroo. It's about the mom."

"All right," Jordan says. "It's your funeral."

"Good luck," I say, and the three of them head off to put the Is Penny A Good Person? test into action. I wish I could help, but Penny can't see me at all today or she might recognize me when she starts dating my dad. All I can do is hide and make some observations.

My friends edge close to Penny, and when they're right next to her, Jordan dodges in front of Keiko and "accidentally trips her." Keiko dramatically falls to the floor, clutching her ankle and yowling. She might be overdoing it a little. Jordan and Miriam crouch down next to her and rub her back.

"I'm *sooooo* sorry," Jordan says. "I didn't mean to hurt you."

Penny looks around, obviously searching for Keiko's parents. When she doesn't see anyone rushing to her rescue, she kneels down next to my friend right away, exactly as I hoped. I give her another point for genuinely caring about other people's children.

"Are you okay?" she asks. Her voice sounds gentle but firm, the kind of tone that says *I can keep calm in a crisis*. It's exactly the kind of voice I'd want to hear if I had actually hurt myself.

"My ankle," Keiko moans. "I think it might be sprained."

"Where are your parents?" Penny asks.

"Her mom's not picking us up until two," Mir says.

Penny turns back to Keiko. "What's your name, honey?"

"Keiko," she says tearfully. I have to admit, she's doing a pretty good job of acting now.

"All right, Keiko. We're going to get you fixed up. I'm sure there's a first aid station somewhere." Penny pulls a zoo map out of her back pocket and unfolds it, and I give her another point for being prepared. "Here, there's one at the office, but it's all the way across the park. Can one of you girls find someone who works here so they can call for a wheelchair?"

"I'll do it," Miriam says, and she scampers off. As she passes me, she gives me a thumbs-up.

"I don't need a wheelchair," moans Keiko.

"You can't possibly walk all the way there with a sprained ankle. Now, let's get you out of the way so you don't get trampled. There's a bench near the sloth cage. Put your arm around my neck, and I'm going to help you get up, okay? Don't put any weight on your bad foot." She turns to Jordan. "Can you wait here for your friend and show her where we are when she gets back?"

I smile to myself—Penny is passing my test with flying colors. I love how she's taking charge of the situation, and she's so focused on Keiko and her "bad ankle" that she hasn't even looked around for my dad in a few minutes. She clearly has her priorities in order: children before romance. Once she's done taking care of Keiko, I'll send her a message and suggest a new time and place to meet. I'm sure she won't mind—I didn't need to worry so much before. Maybe we can all go to the aquarium next weekend, and she and my dad will meet for the first time by the Great Ocean Tank as the sea turtles swim by, and it'll be super romantic, and they'll always buy each other turtle stuff on their anniversaries in honor of that moment, and—

"Kyle," Penny shouts off to her left. "Hey! Kyle!"

For the first time, I notice a boy my age standing in the corner between the pygmy hippo and the snake. He's in a black hoodie and way-too-baggy jeans, and he's wearing a baseball cap pulled low over his eyes and enormous headphones. Two pygmy hippos are nosing at each other in an incredibly cute way in the cage behind him, but his eyes stay glued to his screen. Phone games are fun and everything, but I don't understand people who block everything out *all the time*, especially when there's incredibly cool stuff going on in the real world.

Kyle still hasn't looked up, and Penny sighs and turns to her daughter. "Sarah, can you please go get your brother's attention?"

I watch the girl go over and tap Kyle on the arm, and he shrugs her off like she's a gross bug. She tugs hard on his sleeve, which finally makes him rip off his headphones. "God, *what?*"

"Mom wants you," the girl says. She doesn't look remotely surprised by his violent reaction, which probably mean he treats her like this all the time. *Big* mark in the minus column.

Kyle rolls his eyes so hard I'm pretty sure he can see his own brain. Then he trudges over to Penny and Keiko, headphones dangling from his skinny neck. *"What?"* he says again.

"Watch your sister and brother for a minute, okay?" Penny says. "This girl hurt herself, and I need to find her some help."

"Ugh, fine," grumbles Kyle, and he heads toward the gorilla

enclosure, already looking back down at his phone. He reaches for his headphones, and Penny says, "Headphones off!" without even looking. Kyle sighs like she's asked him to chop a load of firewood.

Penny scoops Keiko off the floor in one smooth motion, and they snuffle-hop in the direction of the sloth cage. The second Penny turns her back, her younger son starts pounding on the glass with both hands again while he lets out another round of monkey shrieks. A bubble of annoyance expands in my chest—I know he's a little kid, but I *hate* when people do that in zoos. I mean, can you imagine if someone pounded on your windows and made faces at you while you were trying to eat and do your homework? So rude.

"Dylan, *stop*," says Sarah, but the boy pounds harder. All the gorillas have moved to the other side of the enclosure, which is exactly what I would do if I were a gorilla. Then Dylan presses his mouth to the glass and starts making fart sounds. When he pulls back to laugh hysterically, a string of spit stretches between the glass and his bottom lip.

"I'm *booooorrrred*," Sarah whines at Kyle.

"Too bad," Kyle says. His thumbs race over the phone screen.

"I want to go see the lions."

"So go," Kyle says. "I don't care."

"But Mom said we had to stay with you."

"Then wait."

"But I want to go *nooowwww*," the girl wails, and it sets my teeth on edge.

"Shut *up*, Sarah." Dylan launches in with another round of pounding, and Kyle shouts, "God, both of you *shut up*! I *hate* you!"

"I hate *you*!" Sarah shrieks, and she shoves him into the glass.

And just like that, I know I can't possibly set Penny up with my dad. Sure, she's competent and gentle and nice, and I feel terrible for having led her on. But it's like Miriam said—my dad has to come first. I need to protect him and make sure he doesn't end up in a bad situation. And I can't possibly think of a worse situation than stepfathering a bunch of monsters.

◆

From: SuperDad_DSC
To: PennyForYrThoughts
Penny,
I'm so sorry to bail on you, but my daughter started throwing up in the car on the way to the zoo. I hope you didn't hang out in the gorilla house too long waiting for me.
Okay, please don't hate me, but . . . I actually don't think we should meet each other after all. I'm not totally sure my daughter is ready for me to start dating yet, and she's pretty stressed out preparing for this dog show she's doing in November, and I really don't want to make her life harder. So I think I'm going to hold off on Head Over Heels for now. You seem awesome, and I hope you find a guy who's as great as you. Seriously, I am really, really, really sorry.
David

From: PennyForYrThoughts
To: SuperDad_DSC
Man, that's such a good reason that I can't even hate you.

— 7 —

I'm pretty sad that the Penny experiment was such a failure,
and the fact that I have to hide my disappointment from my dad all night
and pretend I had a great time at the zoo makes me feel even worse. But
fortunately I don't have too much time to focus on it. We start learning
complicated new choreography for the winter ballet recital on Monday, I
have an essay about *The Giver* due on Thursday, and I spend all my spare
time running patterns with Elvis in the backyard. I barely even have time
to look at Head Over Heels, but when I'm able to sneak a few minutes
here and there, I'm pleased to see that my dad's inbox is bursting with
messages. Maybe the perfect woman is waiting one click away. Until I
have time to go through them carefully, I can hope for the best.

Before I know it, it's Friday night again, and Mom and Krishnan
and I are on the way to Hartford for the dog show Saturday morning,
aka my shot at redemption. We stay at a dog-friendly motel, and Elvis
chooses to sleep on my bed instead of with my mom and stepdad,

which seems like a good omen. He starts out snuggled on my feet, but by morning he has moved up and claimed most of my pillow. I don't really mind, even though his breath smells disgusting; maybe spending so much time with our heads close together will give us that dog-owner mind-meld we haven't been able to master so far. I watch the way his tail wags as I give him his breakfast and take him out to pee, hoping I'll get better at understanding what he's trying to tell me.

As I shower, I run through the judging process in my head three times, making sure I have every step down. I put on the blue dress I wore to my cousin's bar mitzvah in the spring—it's getting tight around my ribs, but Mom has been too busy to take the one Elvis ripped to the tailor. I Velcro the pouch filled with treats onto my arm, then look in the bathroom mirror to get the full effect. The black fabric of the pouch blends into my cardigan sleeve, and the silver designs I made with glitter glue and stick-on rhinestones match the sequins around my sweater's cuffs and hem. This time I'll have plenty of sparkles, like everyone else.

"You've got this," I tell my reflection. "Today is going to be perfect."

This show is a bit smaller than the one we went to a few weeks ago, but there are still a ton of weird things to look at. Between the door and our grooming station, we pass a woman selling gigantic paintings of dogs riding dragons, a guy who will make you a custom doghouse that's a replica of your actual house, and a couple who makes Christmas ornaments out of edible dog biscuits. There are racks upon racks of Halloween costumes; one guy is trying to get a French fries costume onto his German shepherd, and another lady is dressing her pug like a fire hydrant. (My friends and I already have a group costume planned—we're going to be Steven Universe and the Crystal Gems, and Elvis is going to be Steven's pink lion.) People walk around with dog combs sticking out of their ponytails and drool rags trailing from their pockets, and I smile and pat my pouch. I'm totally a real dog show person now.

My stomach rumbles as Mom and Krishnan set up the grooming table, and I ask, "Can I go get some food while you get Elvis ready?"

"Sure," Mom says. "Be quick, though. We're running a little late, and we should head over to your ring at 8:50."

"I will." She hands me a twenty, then gets to work clipping the fur between Elvis's toes as Krishnan blow-dries his tail to make it extra fluffy.

I get bagels for all of us in record time. But on my way back I pass Stan's Smoothie Shack, and even though I know I'm supposed to hurry, I can't resist. Stan's kind of a fixture at dog shows in the northeast, even though he once told me he's secretly a cat person. When he sees me coming, he breaks into a huge smile, his eyes crinkling up so much that it sends wrinkles clear around the sides of his shiny bald head.

"My favorite customer!" he booms, and even though he probably says that to everyone, it makes me feel special. "What'll it be today, Miss Ella?"

"Strawberry mango breeze, please," I tell him. Mom probably won't be thrilled that I'm spending seven dollars on a drink, but Elvis gets treats all day, and I've worked as hard as he has. I deserve a treat too. When I tell Stan I'm actually going *into* the ring today for the first time, he gives me a high five and sprinkles some extra coconut flakes on top of my drink for luck.

I eat my breakfast in a folding chair next to the grooming table and run through everything I have to remember one last time while Mom and Krishnan finish primping Elvis. When they lift him down to the floor, his tail starts swishing back and forth in what I'm pretty sure is his "ready to go" wag. "Time to head over," Krishnan says. "You all set?"

I expect to feel nerves ricocheting around in my stomach—what if today is a repeat of last show's disaster? But I know that's not going to happen. This time I've thought through all the things that could go wrong. I'm totally prepared, and that means everything is going to be fine.

I brush the crumbs off my hands, check my pouch, run a hand over my hair. Everything is in place. I reach into my pocket and apply some lucky watermelon lip gloss, and then I stand up and give my stepdad my most confident smile. "Yup. Ready."

Mom laughs. "Come here, you've got cream cheese on your face. Let me—"

I step toward her, and my foot hits my enormous smoothie, which is sitting on the floor next to my chair. It topples, and I gasp and jump out of the way as a slushy strawberry lake spreads across the floor. Elvis is immediately under my feet, lapping up my drink like he's been in the desert with no water for weeks. He's so fast that it's almost all gone before any of us is able to grab his collar and pull him away.

"Elvis, *no*!" I shout at him. "*Bad* boy!" He just gazes up at me lovingly and licks his chops, his nose all sticky with strawberry. His tail is going absolutely insane.

"I'm so sorry," I say as Krishnan swoops in with a wet wash-cloth. "It's all strawberries and bananas and mangoes, so it won't make him sick. Should I—"

"Run to the bathroom and get some paper towels to clean up the floor," he says. "It's okay, but we have to hurry or we're going to miss your ring time."

I run, my stomach knotting and my pouch flapping against my arm. I'm going to have to put an extra Velcro strap on this thing—I didn't account for having to dash around with it on. It makes me wonder if there are other things I didn't think of.

Elvis's muzzle isn't quite dry by the time we make it to the ring, but at least we manage to arrive on time. We plant ourselves at the end of the line behind a girl with a really cute Westie, and I try to calm my racing heart as I rubber band Elvis's show number around my arm below my treat pouch. Fortunately I don't recognize any of the kids from the show two weeks ago, which means nobody here has seen my underwear. The judge hasn't even arrived yet, and I'm grateful for the time to catch my breath. The dash across the convention center actually seems to have been good for Elvis—he's not doing that nervous leash-tugging thing from last time—and I tell myself everything is okay. Sure, we had a little hiccup, but it's over now. And Elvis got some extra vitamin C, which means he won't get . . . scurvy? Is that the thing you get on ships?

After a few minutes of waiting, I'm feeling pretty calm again. But then we keep waiting, and we wait some more, and fifteen min-utes later, the judge still hasn't arrived. Now I'm getting seriously annoyed. Why did we bother to rush when it wasn't even necessary? There would have been time to wash Elvis much more thoroughly.

There are probably still sticky strawberry spots on him, and I'll get points off when the judge finds them.

But then something much worse happens: Elvis starts shifting from side to side in this very specific way. It isn't his nervous tug or his excited sway; this is what Krishnan refers to as the pee-pee dance.

"No, no, no, no," I whisper. "Just a little longer, buddy. You can wait, right?" The last time someone took him out was this morning before we got in the car—ordinarily he'd be able to hold it way longer than that. But ordinarily he doesn't drink thirty-two-ounce smoothies.

I glance over my shoulder, trying to find the nearest exit; maybe I can take him out and come back before the judge even gets here. But of course that's the moment she finally decides to show up. She's about my grandma's age, and she's wearing this totally over-the-top jacket covered in green and purple sequins. At least she'll probably appreciate my bedazzled treat pouch.

The steward calls us into the ring, and as we line up along the low plastic fence, Elvis's dance speeds up, and I feel my first real spark of nerves. He looks like I felt that time we got stuck in horrible traffic on the way back from a show in Maine and I had to pee on the shoulder of the road while Mom shielded me with a picnic blanket. I pull a treat out of my pouch and feed it to him, hoping it'll distract him, but it only works for about five seconds, and then he goes right back to shifting.

"Once around all together, not too fast," says the judge. She doesn't sound mean, but she's stern, like she's not going to cut us any slack.

The Westie in front of us has much shorter legs than Elvis, so I let them get ahead of us, and then I tell my dog, "Come on!" in the most authoritative voice I can manage. I've been practicing giving him commands in exactly the right tone, and I must sound super in charge today, because he seems to forget about his discomfort for a second and does what I say. Off we go around the ring. I hold the leash away from my body and try to jog at the perfect speed so that he's trotting but not running. Once we're moving, I start feeling less jittery, and I can tell Elvis does too—maybe running will distract him from his bladder in a way treats can't. Mom and Krishnan nod approvingly.

One step down, three to go. Maybe things are going to be fine after all.

The judge begins her exams with the first dog in line, a tall, skinny, long-haired one that I'm pretty sure is an Afghan hound. I hope she'll hurry, but instead she's really slow and thorough, and by the time she's done looking at him, Elvis is fidgeting in a pretty major way. I make eye contact with my stepdad and try to send him telepathic distress signals—*Is there some sort of trick to make dogs hold their pee? A pressure point I can squeeze or something?* But he clearly doesn't get the message, because he just gives me a thumbs-up and snaps a picture of us with his phone.

The next ten minutes are agonizing. Elvis spends them shifting back and forth, and I spend them repeating *Please don't pee, please don't pee* in my head while I feed him treat after treat. Thinking about peeing reminds me of all the smoothie *I* drank, and after a while I'm honestly not sure either of us is going to get through this competition without an exploded bladder.

And then it's finally, *finally* our turn, and the judge waves me forward. I lead Elvis over to her and arrange his feet and head and tail in a perfect stack, exactly like the picture in the junior showmanship judging guide. It takes me longer than it took my competitors, since this is my first time in the ring, but the judge waits patiently. When we're ready, I dig another treat out of my pouch and hold it above Elvis's nose, and amazingly enough, he lifts his head and stands perfectly still. He's done this literally hundreds more times than I have, and his training kicks in regardless of the circumstances.

You can do it, Elvis, I think. *Just a little longer.*

The judge feels the shape of his skull, checks his teeth, runs her hands down his chest and front legs, inspects the angle of his shoulders, and tests the springiness of his ribs. I pray she doesn't put her hands anywhere near his bladder. But everything goes fine, and when she's finished, she gives Elvis a friendly pat on the butt, and I finally exhale. Two steps down, two to go.

"Down and back, please," the judge says.

It's not a very big ring, so it barely takes Elvis and me any time at all to run across the square on a diagonal and back again, which lets the judge see him move from the front and the rear. Elvis trots along beside me with his tongue out, and when people clap for us, I realize I'm actually enjoying myself. I know I should be embarrassed when I hear a "Woo!" in what is unmistakably my mom's voice, but instead it makes me happy.

The judge smiles when we return and says, "Thank you. Right around, please."

I smile back—trotting around two sides of the square and straight down the middle on the diagonal is all that stands between us and victory. We did it. My dress isn't ripped. I didn't trip over my own feet. The pouch worked great. Smoothie-thief Elvis kept it together and behaved pretty much perfectly, and I don't think the judge found any strawberry goo on him. I know dog shows aren't beauty contests, especially not for junior handling, but I personally think he's the prettiest dog in the ring, and that definitely can't hurt. I might actually have this in the bag.

I finally let myself relax a little.

And that's when Elvis decides to relax a lot.

I've never actually seen someone open the valve on a fire hydrant, but the stream of pee that comes out of Elvis gives me a pretty good idea of what that might look like. In a matter of seconds, there's a lake on the floor . . . and on my nice patent leather competition shoes . . . and on the judge's sparkly green mermaid shoes. She leaps backward like she's never seen a dog go to the bathroom before. In any other situation, it would be hilarious to watch an old lady jump so high—everyone in the crowd is roaring. But it's a lot less funny when your dreams of a first-place ribbon are melting away like an ice cube in a mug of hot tea.

"Oh my god, I'm so, so sorry," I say to the judge. She doesn't yell at me or anything, but she doesn't say it's okay, either. She fishes a tissue out of her pocket and dabs at her pee-stained sparkly toes.

Standing there on the other end of my gushing dog's leash is 100 percent mortifying, especially because he doesn't even have the decency to look ashamed of himself. But it's not like I can stop him once he starts, so I have to wait it out, cheeks flaming, while everyone around me laughs at the never-ending stream. At least my underwear isn't on display this time.

So much for thinking of every possible problem.

— 8 —

My friends aren't available for an EVGAP the next day, but they
send lots of sympathetic texts and funny gifs, and Miriam offers to
come over and join my dad and me for Italian Food Sunday. Her
parents aren't very good cooks, so it's possible she's mostly interested in the lasagna, but I know having her there will make me feel
better regardless. I try to get Dad to take me to mini golf during the
day to cheer me up, but he says he has too many chores to do, even
though he spends basically every second that he's not working doing
stuff around the house. Knowing that the pre-divorce version of
Dad totally would've taken me makes me even sadder. I *really* have to
find him someone else to date soon. Both of us would be so much
happier if he could go back to being his old self.

Mir arrives a few minutes before dinner, and when Dad goes
into the kitchen to take the lasagna out of the oven, she whispers,
"When we sit down, ask me what I did this weekend."

"Why, what did you do?"

"Ask me in front of your dad," she says. "Trust me. I'm going to lay some groundwork."

I have no idea what she's talking about, but Mir never steers me wrong, so I just shrug. And then Dad calls, "Girls! Dinner!" and we follow the tantalizing smell of sauce into the kitchen.

Miriam dives into her lasagna with the same enthusiasm as Elvis with a spilled smoothie. "OMG, Mr. Cohen," she says, rolling her eyes back with happiness. "This is, like, the best thing I've ever eaten. You should quit your job and be a professional chef. The world's taste buds need you."

"Seriously, Dad, this is awesome," I say.

Dad beams. "Thank you. I'm so glad you like it. I put butternut squash in it."

Mir nods hard. "Genius. I *love* butternut squash."

She stuffs another huge bite into her mouth, and I wait until she swallows before I ask, "So, what've you been up to this weekend, Mir?"

"My cousins and I went shopping for bridesmaid's dresses with my uncle's fiancée, Kathryn! She's so, *so* cool."

"That sounds fun," I say. I work hard to make my voice sound totally casual, but I kind of want to leap up and hug her. I've been trying to figure out how to drop some hints that I'd be cool with Dad starting to date again, but I haven't found a good way to bring it up.

"I've never been in a wedding before, and everyone says people are supposed to turn into bridezillas when they get married, but she's not like that at all," Mir continues. "Nobody could agree on the best style for the dresses, so she said everyone can wear whatever they want as long as it's the right shade of purple."

"Nice," I say. "How long have she and your uncle been together?"

Mir licks sauce off her fork. "Mm, a couple years, I guess? My uncle got divorced when I was probably . . . I don't know, seven or eight? My mom never thought he'd find anyone else, but Kathryn joined the choir at his temple a few years later, and *bam*, they liked each other right away. I guess you never know when or where you're going to meet someone awesome."

I peek at my dad, and even though he's not asking any questions, it seems like he's paying attention. I really hope he's thinking about his own potential post-divorce love life, not the one Mom already has. "Do your cousins like her?" I ask.

"Yeah, they get along great. Shira especially. I think she was nervous when Uncle Danny started dating again, but now she and Kathryn even do stuff together without him. Kind of like you and—" I shoot her a warning look, and Mir catches herself before she says Krishnan's name. "*Anyway*, Shira totally loves her now. I'm jealous that she has this woman she's super close to but who isn't her mom, you know?"

"That sounds pretty great." I wait for my dad to say something, but he just sits there forking up his food, a slight frown on his face. Mir has probably given him enough to think about, so I give him permission to tune out by asking, "Do you have pictures of the dresses?"

Mir pulls out her phone to show me, and the rest of dinner passes pretty uneventfully. Dad asks Miriam if she's excited about her bat mitzvah, which is a few months before mine, and we talk about this new reality show called *Chow Hound*, where people compete to make the best gourmet meals for dogs. Dad has made ten-minute tiramisu for dessert, and even though I feel like I might pop at the seams, I still manage to put away a pretty generous helping. When Mir's mom texts that she's out front, it's a huge effort to get up and walk her to the door.

"Thanks for saying all that stuff to my dad," I whisper as I hug her goodbye. "You were so sneaky!"

"Of course," she says. "We're going to make this work—you'll see." She gives me one last squeeze, shouts an extra thank-you to my dad, and then she's gone.

I linger by the door for a few minutes, watching her mom's car pull away. I'm nervous for the conversation I'm about to have with Dad—I'm not nearly as slick as Mir, and I'm not sure I'm going to be able to make the things I want to say sound natural. And it's not like I *have* to say any of them right now. But Miriam served me the ball so perfectly that I can't possibly ignore it.

I go into the kitchen, where Dad is loading the dishwasher, and lean against the counter behind him. "So, Miriam's new aunt Kathryn sounds cool," I say. "She seems to really like her."

"Mmm-hmm," Dad says.

I take a deep breath—it's now or never. "Have you . . . have you ever . . ." I start, but that doesn't seem like the right beginning to the sentence, so I backtrack and try again. "Um, do you think you might consider maybe trying to date again?"

Dad shuts the faucet off and turns around to face me. His eyes are big and soft, almost like he feels sorry for me. "Ellabee, you don't have to worry about that. I know how hard it was for you when Mom started dating, and I've got no plans to do it anytime soon."

It was a little hard for me at first when Krishnan came into the picture—Mom and Dad had only been divorced a few months, so everything was new and fresh and weird, and it was a lot of change all at once. But it's been years since then, and now I know how great having a stepparent can be. "No, no, I'm not *worried* about it," I say. "I actually wouldn't mind at all if you went on some dates. I mean, if you wanted to. You don't need to hold off because of me, is what I'm saying, if that's what you're doing. Seriously. I just want you to be happy."

"You have *never* kept me from being happy, and you never will," Dad says. "I'm happiest when I'm with you, sweetheart. To be honest, I don't have much interest in dating right now. All I need is lots of hang-out time with my number one girl." He comes over and kisses the top of my head. "I don't ever want you to feel like you're not enough to make me happy."

I want him to have *lots* of things that make him happy again; that's the entire point. "I love hanging out with you too, obviously," I say. "But it wouldn't have to be one or the other, right? I'm only here half the time, and I want your life to be awesome *all* the time. Maybe there are tons of amazing women around, and you're missing out because you're not looking. The perfect person could be sitting in her house right now thinking about how she wishes she had a really cool bald boyfriend who makes great pasta."

Dad chuckles. "If I ever decide I want to date again, I'm sure there will be plenty of women then too. They're not going anywhere."

"But what if they are? What if the good ones are all taken by then?"

His eyebrows crinkle. "Sweetheart, where is all this coming from? I've never heard you talk about this before." He's giving me this weird look that makes me realize I've totally overdone it.

I shrug in a way that I hope looks casual. "I don't know. Nowhere. All the stuff Miriam said, I guess. I thought it could be cool. And . . . I don't know, I like hanging out with Krishnan. So I thought it could be fun having someone around here too. It only seems fair, you know?"

Dad's jaw tightens, and I wonder if I've made a mistake by mentioning Krishnan. But his eyes also look steelier, the way they get when we're playing cards and his competitive spirits kicks in, so maybe it was exactly the right thing to say. When he told me he thought I should quit the dog show a couple weeks ago, it only made me more determined to do it, and I definitely got that quality from him.

"That's very selfless of you," Dad says. "Thank you. But I really don't want you to worry about this. I know you're stressed about other things, so you can put this out of your mind."

Of course, the fact that he doesn't seem willing to date is one of the things that's stressing me out the most, but it's not like I can tell him that. So I say, "Okay. But if I *promise* I'm not stressed, will you promise me something too?"

"Sure," he says, slinging an arm around my shoulders.

I snuggle into his side so I don't have to look at his face. "If you *happen* to meet someone really awesome, will you give her a chance and not write her off because you think it might upset me?"

Dad's chest moves up and down under my cheek as he sighs. "Okay," he says. "I promise. But don't hold your breath. It's not like I meet awesome single women all the time."

I smile into his T-shirt. "True," I say. "But you never know when coincidence might strike."

To: SuperDad_DSC
From: DrownedInMoonlight

Hey, SuperDad! Just stumbled across your profile, and I think we might be a good match. I worked in advertising for a little while before I went to law school; it's a tough industry, and I admire you for sticking it out. I've definitely seen that granola ad you mentioned, and I remember thinking it was clever. I'd love to meet the man behind the idea. Any interest in grabbing a drink next weekend?

xo,

Linda

To: DrownedInMoonlight
From: SuperDad_DSC

Hi, Linda! I'm glad you liked the Granolatastic ads! You don't say much about yourself in your profile! Do you have any kids? Any pets? Have you ever been married? Do you like being a lawyer? Hope you're having a good day!

David

To: SuperDad_DSC
From: DrownedInMoonlight

Hey, glad to hear back from you! Totally reasonable that you'd want to get to know me better before going out. I've never been married, and I don't have any kids, though I'm close to my four nieces and nephews. I haven't decided whether I want kids of my own, but I've always thought I might like to adopt someday. I have an adorable dog named Patti, and I'm thinking about getting another one. You wouldn't believe how much time I waste on PetFinder. Are you a dog person? I've been doing intellectual property law for eight years now, and I really love it! I hope that doesn't make me sound stodgy, because I'm actually pretty fun. :) You can find out much more about me if you meet me for a drink this coming Sunday.

xo,

Linda

To: DrownedInMoonlight
From: SuperDad_DSC

Dear Linda,

Your dog sounds really cute. I'm a huge dog person. Do you know what breed Patti is? Are there any specific dogs on PetFinder that you have your eye on? What are your nieces' and nephews' names and ages? Do they live nearby? Do you spend a lot of time with them? What are they interested in? Also, are you a Sox fan? If you're into the Yankees, we definitely can't date. Also, are you gluten-free? I make a lot of Italian food. I've never tried any of it with gluten-free pasta.

David

To: SuperDad_DSC
From: DrownedInMoonlight

I love gluten, but I'm not into baseball. How about I'll show you pictures of all the nieces and nephews and dogs when we get together? You don't need to know *everything* about me before we meet, do you?

xo,

Linda

To: DrownedInMoonlight
From: SuperDad_DSC

No, you're right. Let's hang out this weekend. Can you meet me at Little Pete's Italian Kitchen at the mall? It's on the second floor, by the Sunglass Hut and the Hot Topic. I know it's not exactly the most romantic place ever, but my daughter will be with me that day, and I thought she could shop while we hang out. Plus they actually have really good garlic bread.

To: SuperDad_DSC
From: DrownedInMoonlight

Um . . . okay, I guess?

To: DrownedInMoonlight
From: SuperDad_DSC

Cool. And can I ask you one more thing? I still feel kind of strange about this whole online dating thing, so can we not discuss Head Over Heels at all and pretend we're meeting for the first time that night?

To: *SuperDad_DSC*

From: *DrownedInMoonlight*

All right, I'll be honest—that's kind of weird, after you asked me a million questions. But I guess we all have our quirks. I'll pretend the best I can. See you there.

— 9 —

Getting Dad into position for his sneak-attack date with Linda

the following Sunday isn't quite as easy as I expect. I manage to drag him to the mall by convincing him to take me to a movie, but the only show that ends at the right time is this stupid one about a professional skateboarder who fights crime, so I have to pretend I'm excited about that. The movie is way too long and incredibly boring, and I'm half asleep by the time it finally gets out at 6:30. I stumble to the bathroom, splash some freezing-cold water on my face to shock myself into alertness, then use a safety pin I brought to rip a jagged hole in the knee of my jeans. Then I paste an exasperated look on my face—not hard after watching the same skateboard trick four hundred times—and go find Dad.

"Look what happened when I crouched down to tie my shoe!" I huff.

"You're probably growing," he says. "We'll have to get you some new clothes soon."

"I mean . . . we're at the mall right now. Do you think maybe I could get some jeans before we go?"

He checks the time on his phone. "It's kind of late, kiddo. We're not going to end up eating for another hour as it is."

"But I'm not hungry after all that popcorn. I don't care if we eat right away."

Dad sighs. "Can't Mom bring you back here sometime next week?"

I do my best Wonder Woman impression—hands on hips, chin lifted, staring him down. "What are you saying, Dad? That it's the *woman's* job to do the shopping?"

And that does it, just like I knew it would; Dad's as much of a feminist as Mom and me. "Fine," he says. "But try to be quick, okay?"

"Definitely. You don't even have to come into the stores with me. Why don't you give me some money and hang out at Little Pete's? Get a snack and relax." I want to say *You might even find someone interesting to talk to*, but I don't want him to get suspicious.

"Hmm," Dad says. "They *do* have weirdly good garlic bread."

"Yeah, they totally do. Come on, let's go." I turn around like it's all decided, and to my relief, Dad follows me.

Little Pete's Italian Kitchen really does have good garlic bread, but I chose it for Dad's date because of the layout. There's only one "official" entrance, but since the restaurant is right in the middle of the third floor, between the two rows of stores, it's possible to enter on either side as long as the staff isn't paying attention. It's kind of a weird place—there are giant jugs of olive oil and wine everywhere, red-and-white-checked tablecloths that brush the floor, and candles on every table, even though the flickering shadows are completely washed out by the fluorescent ceiling lights. It's like someone was on the way to deliver a fancy restaurant to Rome, stopped at the mall for frozen yogurt on the way, and left it there by mistake.

It's 6:52 when I leave Dad at the end of the bar, facing the door, checking e-mail on his phone and awaiting a plate of garlic bread. I make sure he watches me leave—I even give him a jaunty wave when I get to the entrance—and walk off down the hall toward Gap. Then I circle around to the back of the restaurant, which has a sign on the gate that says STAFF ENTRANCE ONLY: PLEASE USE DOOR ACROSS FROM SUNGLASS HUT.

The restaurant isn't busy, but luckily there's a family with three kids near the front, and they're all the distraction I need. It only takes three minutes before one of them knocks over his milk and starts crying, and a bunch of servers swoop in with napkins and new milk and a replacement bread basket. I take the opportunity to push through the staff gate, do an undignified crouch-run across the path to the kitchen, and dive under the empty table right behind my dad. When I use my safety pin to make a tiny tear in the tablecloth and squint through it like I'm using a microscope, I can see what's happening at the bar.

I have to say, I'm feeling pretty pleased with myself. This time I've thoroughly vetted my dad's date, so there won't be any surprises like there were with Penny. Plus my dad is actually *here* this time, so I don't have to feel bad about some poor woman thinking she's been stood up. As long as Linda doesn't mention the dating site, she and my dad can get to know each other naturally, and I know they'll both like what they find. I'll wait right here until I see them exchange numbers, and then I'll text my dad, tell him I'm done shopping, and ask him to meet me at the entrance.

Right on cue, a woman approaches the bar. She's got dark hair that falls to the middle of her back—I can never get mine that shiny, no matter what shampoo I use—and she's wearing a red sweater and skinny jeans that are exactly the kind I would want if I were actually shopping for jeans. When she walks up to my dad and slides onto the stool next to his, my heart leaps—it's totally her! I hadn't realized it until now, but part of me was terrified she was going to bail. She did *not* seem excited about Little Pete's.

Linda turns so I can see her face. She's even prettier in person than she was in her picture, and I cross my fingers and hope my dad agrees and falls head over heels for her.

"I hear this place has really good garlic bread," she says with a twinkle in her eye. She has an accent that sounds like my Spanish teacher's, but not as strong.

My dad looks up from his phone, and even though I can't see his face, I can picture the polite confusion that must be there. "Yeah, it does," he says. "I was just saying the same thing to my daughter."

"It's nice to see you in person," says Linda, and she leans toward him like she's about to kiss him on the cheek.

My dad recoils. "I'm sorry, do we know each other?"

"Oh, *right*. I forgot we were doing that. Sorry." Linda sits back and extends her hand. "I'm Linda."

"David," my dad says, and I'm relieved to see that he takes her hand, even if he seems hesitant.

"Very nice to meet you for the *first time in any context*, David," Linda purrs. For a second I'm afraid he's going to turn away like he did that time a homeless guy came up to us in the Public Garden and tried to give us pamphlets about the Great Lizard God, but instead he just says a bewildered, "You too."

A server slides a menu across the bar to Linda. "Can I get you a drink to start?" he asks.

"I'll have a Malbec, please," she says. Then she turns to my dad. "Tell me about yourself, David. What do you do for work?" She flips her hair over her shoulder, leans on her elbow, and looks at him like he's the most interesting person in the world. Total heartthrob move. Nice work, Linda.

"Um, I work in advertising?" my dad starts. But I don't hear the rest, because there's a loud scraping sound right next to my head, then another. I instinctively duck and cover, afraid the table is about to collapse . . . and then I realize that something much worse is happening.

People are pulling out the chairs on either side of me.

People are *sitting down at my table*.

There wasn't a lot of room under here to begin with, and now that there are two pairs of legs crowding in on me, I have to pull my knees up to my chest in order to fit. Both pairs of feet look like they belong to women; one is in glittery silver flats, and the other is in red Converse sneakers with rainbow laces. I try to be as small as possible; if one of them discovers me, she'll probably make a scene, and my dad will notice, and the game will be up. There's no plausible excuse for me being here besides *I was spying on the date you didn't know you were on*.

Come to think of it, that's not very plausible either.

The Converse feet are exactly where I need to sit in order to see through my peephole, and I'm too afraid to tear another hole in case the diners notice me tugging on their tablecloth. I strain my ears and try and pick up what Linda and my dad are saying—I'm able to catch the words "lawyer" and "boss" and "annoying"—but then the women connected to the feet start talking, and it totally drowns them out.

"Are you seriously breaking up with me at *Little Pete's*?" hisses Converse. "This is worse than the time I got dumped at the Cheesecake Factory."

Silver sighs. "I mean, we have to talk about this sometime. Does it really matter where? It's not like there's a good place to do it."

"Pretty much anywhere is better than the *mall*! There are a million people listening! Even if you don't love me anymore, the least you could do is respect my privacy!"

"This isn't about whether I love you or not!" says Silver. "It's about the fact that I'm being transferred to Hong Kong for three years. I'm not saying we're absolutely one hundred percent done forever. I'm saying maybe we should consider seeing other people while I'm gone."

"No, I get it," says Converse. "You're saying I'm not good enough to hold your attention unless I'm right in front of you every second."

Oh god, this is so, so bad. How is my dad supposed to slip into a romantic mood without realizing it when another couple is breaking up eight feet away?

"You're *never* going to be in front of me," says Silver. "You won't even get on a plane long enough to visit my parents in Florida, so how are you going to get to Asia? It's not like I can hop back to Boston every month. What am I supposed to do?"

"If you really loved me, you'd make it work," Converse says.

"If *you* really loved *me*, you'd take a sleeping pill and get on a plane!"

"You know I can't!"

"And I can't do all the work in this relationship!"

Converse stretches out her leg and kicks me hard in the hip, and it takes everything I have not to yelp. She pulls her foot back quickly and tucks it under her chair. "Sorry," she says.

"I'm sorry too," says Silver, misunderstanding. "I wish things were different. You know I do. But I can't turn down this job. I've been waiting for this my entire life."

"I've been waiting for *you* my entire life," sniffles Converse.

And then I hear Linda's raised voice. "Okay, this make-believe thing is getting ridiculous. I'm impressed with your commitment to the whole 'Let's pretend we just met' bit, but do we seriously have to have *every* conversation all over again?"

The women at my table go silent, and Silver's legs shift to the side—I can tell she's twisting around in her seat to look at Linda and my dad.

"I'm sorry, but I honestly don't know what you're talking about," my dad says. "Have we met before? I feel like I'd remember that, but I—"

"I know you feel weird about the website, but you can't pretend it doesn't exist." Linda's voice is getting higher and shriller by the minute. "If you felt that awkward, you shouldn't have signed up in the first place."

"What website?" my dad asks. He sounds completely baffled. Man, I thought I was being so clever with the whole *Let's not talk about Head Over Heels* thing.

Linda says something else, but I don't catch it because Converse says, "Wow, that couple over there is even more dysfunctional than we are."

"I really think you must have me confused for someone else," my dad is saying.

"How could I have you confused for someone else?" Linda

snaps. "You're the one who asked me to meet *you* here!"

"I didn't ask anyone to meet me here! I didn't even know I'd be here until fifteen minutes ago. I'm just waiting for my daughter while she shops for jeans!"

It's quiet for a minute—the only sound is Converse whispering, "What is going *on* over there?"—and when Linda starts talking again, her voice is low and dangerous. "Oh. I see what's going on here."

My heart starts pounding. Linda can't possibly know I made my dad's account, can she? If she tells him that, she's going to ruin absolutely *everything*.

But then she says, "You're one of those jerks who responds to so many women at a time that you literally can't keep track of them all. You probably didn't even remember *who* you were supposed to meet tonight. Do you bring all your dates to Little Pete's, David? Such a class act."

"I don't . . . ," my dad sputters. "I've seriously never— What are you—?"

Linda cuts him off. "How many women do you reply to at a time? Twenty? Fifty? I read an article about this, how guys send the same message to huge batches of women at once, hoping it'll raise their odds. Well, I'm not here for that, David. I'm looking for a real relationship with someone who actually cares about *me*."

"Oh *snap*," says Converse in a low voice.

I'm terrified Linda is going to pull out her phone, open the Head Over Heels app, and shove it in my dad's face to prove that they really did have an e-mail exchange, and when I hear boot heels clicking toward me instead, I almost faint with relief. "You can pay for my wine," she says as she passes my table. "You owe it to me. This is the tackiest place

I've ever seen." Then the heels click past me and out the door.

It's quiet for a minute, and I hug my knees and bury my face in them. I desperately want to peek at my dad to see if he's upset, but he's probably just totally confused. I'm sure he thinks he spent the last five minutes being yelled at by a crazy stranger. It's like the lizard gods all over again.

"Oh man," says Converse. "Is that what we sounded like a few minutes ago?"

"God, I hope not," says Silver. "You were right—Little Pete's is a terrible place for a breakup."

I breathe a sigh of relief—these women are going to leave without even getting drinks, and I'll finally be able to unfold my limbs.

And then Silver says, "Let's get some pasta and talk about other stuff, and we'll finish this conversation when we get home. Maybe there's a solution we haven't thought of. We'll try to work it out. Okay?"

"Okay," Converse says. "Thanks, sweetie." She extends her leg again, and I manage to scoot backward just in time. Her ankle nestles against Silver's, who doesn't pull away, and it cuts my space under the table by a third. I fold my elbows and knees in as close to my body as I can, afraid to breathe too deeply. One of my feet is starting to fall asleep.

My phone buzzes, and Converse says, "Is that yours?"

"It doesn't matter," Silver says. "I'll deal with it later."

So slowly it's painful, I manage to inch my phone out of my back pocket. On the screen is a message from my dad.

Dad: You almost done shopping?
Me: It might be a while. Everything's kind of a tight fit.

— 10 —

I'm still grumpy by the time I get to science class the next morning. I know I need to shake off my disappointment and get back to work—if I want to be a scientist, I have to accept the fact that experiments can fail hundreds of times before you find a method that finally works. But I don't have time for hundreds of failed trials. I only have five weeks left before the National Dog Show, and I need my dad to turn back into himself by then.

"Were you really crammed under that table for forty minutes?" Jordan asks.

"*Yes*. And they were holding hands right by my face almost the entire time. I kept having to dodge out of the way."

"That sounds awful," Miriam says. "And I'm so sorry it didn't work out with your dad and Linda."

"At least those women didn't drop a fork and poke your eye out or something," Jordan says. "Can you imagine if they'd had to call an ambulance? 'Miss, what were you doing under this table?' 'Oh, nothing, doctor, just accidentally spying on this date while trying to spy on *that* date. . . .'"

That finally gets a laugh out of me, and I'm feeling a little better by the time Ms. McKinnon arrives. Today her hair is up in a bunch of complicated braids wrapped around her head like a crown, and her shirt has two dinosaurs and the words CURSE YOUR SUDDEN BUT INEVITABLE BETRAYAL! I have no idea what that's supposed to mean, but I'm sure it's a reference to something cool. Everything about Ms. McKinnon is a reference to something cool.

"Scientists!" she announces. "This is a very exciting morning. Because this morning, we're going to start brainstorming about *your science fair projects*!"

A bunch of kids roll their eyes or groan—Ethan Fenton actually puts his head down on his desk like a toddler who doesn't want to eat his carrots—but my heart does a little leap. I *love* the science fair.

"I know it's early," Ms. McKinnon says over the moans. "The actual fair won't happen until December. But as seventh graders, you'll be focusing on the life sciences, and when you're doing an experiment that involves plants or insects or fish, it can be a while before there are any significant results. So you're going to have to get the ball rolling now."

As Ms. McKinnon talks us through the requirements for our projects, I briefly consider writing up a report on the scientific methods I'm using to find my dad love. But I'm pretty sure she wouldn't go for it, not to mention the fact that I wouldn't be able to invite either of my parents to the science fair—it's already going to be complicated enough designating different hours for Dad and Krishnan to come.

Ms. McKinnon announces that we have today to think and talk to her about potential projects, and it only takes a few minutes before I have another idea that relates to someone I love: Elvis. For a while now, I've been trying to figure out whether his different tail wag patterns correspond to different kinds of happiness, and this is the perfect opportunity to gather some data about what dogs are really telling us. Mom, Krishnan, and I are going to a dog show in Rhode Island next weekend, and I decide I'll test a bunch of dogs and see if they wag their tails differently when they see their favorite snacks, their owners, or their favorite toys. When Ms. McKinnon comes around to our lab table to check in, she's excited about my idea. The two of us figure out how to conduct the experiment in the most scientific way possible, and by the time she moves on to Keiko, who wants to investigate whether cats have dominant paws, I'm bursting with ideas.

When Ms. McKinnon leaves, Miriam beckons us close. "All right," she says. "Time to figure out where we're going wrong with your dad's potential girlfriends."

I sigh and push my notebook away. "So the problem with Penny was that I didn't find out enough about her online. I suggested a meeting way too early, and then when I didn't like her kids, I had to shut it down, and she thought my dad had bailed on her, which was super unfair."

"Those kids were monsters," says Jordan.

"But then I overcorrected with Linda and tried to make her tell me too *much* about herself in e-mails, and it weirded her out. And then it backfired even more when she thought my dad was asking her the same questions all over again. She said some pretty mean stuff to him, but I feel kind of bad for her anyway, you know? Can you imagine if you went on a date and you thought the other person had forgotten who you were?"

Keiko nods. "Yeah, that'd be super weird."

"I can't figure out what the right amount of messaging is," I say. "I don't want to miss an important piece of information and set my dad up with someone terrible. But I also can't e-mail a woman a million times and then make her forget I did it."

"I wish there were a way to erase someone's memory," Keiko says.

"That'd be great. But I'm not Hermione Granger."

Miriam chews on the end of her pen, a sure sign that she's coming up with an idea. Finally she says, "What if you didn't e-mail the women at all?"

"Isn't talking to people online the entire point of online dating?" asks Keiko.

"That's the thing, though. What if you could meet someone in real life and scope her out, *then* introduce her to your dad? Like, say you found someone who's a waitress. You could go to her restaurant and sit in her section, and then you could 'get sick' and ask her to stay with you until your dad picks you up. Then you could introduce them and tell him what a good job she did of taking care of you and see if they hit it off. Or you could find someone who's a tutor and have her come to your house to help you with math, and then she and your dad could talk."

"Excuse you," I say. "I have a ninety-eight in math."

Mir rolls her eyes. "That was just an example. You know what I mean."

Her plan is a pretty good one, actually. It's basically what I tried to do with Dad and Ms. McKinnon, except this time I'd know beyond a doubt that my target was single and looking for a boyfriend. And it would be nicer for the woman, too; she'd actually get to *meet* my dad before she had to decide if she wanted to go out with him. Sure, this plan would require deviousness, but it also seems way more fair to everyone. And let's be honest—I spent last night hiding under a table as people played footsie two feet from my face. It can't possibly get worse than that.

"I like this," I say. "This is good. I'll go through some more profiles tonight."

I pull my notebook back toward me and jot down Mir's dating plan alongside my notes about the science fair, feeling pretty optimistic for the first time all day. Both procedures seem solid, and I'm confident I can pull them off. And if I'm lucky, they'll both yield plenty of results.

— 11 —

When I get home from ballet later that afternoon, all I want to do is go online, sort through my dad's new likes on Head Over Heels, and get started on my brand-new experimental method. But we have plans to go over to Krishnan's sister's house for dinner, and I barely have time to take a shower before my stepdad calls me downstairs. We visit Anjali pretty often, but for some reason Krishnan seems extra excited today, and he keeps making that special, weighted kind of eye contact with my mom where it seems like words are flying back and forth between their heads. It always made me feel kind of sick when Mom and Dad did that, since it usually meant they were in the middle of a big fight they didn't want me to know about. When Mom and Krishnan do it, I never worry, but I'm still pretty curious about what's happening.

They do it again one more time when we get in the car, and then Krishnan turns around to look at me, a huge grin plastered across his face. He's one of those people with such an enormous bright smile that it makes you smile back every time, even if you don't really feel like it. "I have a surprise for you," he says to me. "A really good one."

"What is it?" I don't really love surprises—even if I know it's something good, not having a sense of what's coming makes me a little nervous.

"I can't tell you yet," he says. "But it's at Anjali's, so you'll know soon. We'll tell you all together when we get there."

The car ride to my aunt's house is less than ten minutes, but even thirty seconds seems endless when you know there's something mysterious waiting at the end of it. I sit on the edge of my seat all the way there, then jump out of the car before Krishnan has even finished turning it off and run across the lawn to the bright blue house with the white shutters. When Anjali opens the door, I crash into her and give her a huge hug.

"Hey, babe," she says into my hair—Anjali calls everyone babe for some reason. "I made your favorite saag paneer."

My stomach rumbles; I'm always especially starving after ballet, and Anjali's cooking is *so good*. I can't get enough of the homemade cheese she puts in the saag.

"Awesome," I say. "Krishnan says you guys have a surprise for me?"

Anjali's eyes light up. "We certainly do. Come on in, and we'll tell you all about it."

I step inside Anjali's living room, which is painted a sunny yellow—each room in her house is a different bright shade. A wave of amazing savory smells washes over me, and Anjali's Welsh springer spaniel, Minerva, bounds out of the kitchen and greets me by planting both front paws on my chest. She's super well-behaved at shows, but at home she's basically a giant, hyper ball of love. "Hey, sweet girl," I croon, and she gives my cheek a tongue bath while I scratch the scruff of her neck. She's got more white patches on her head than Elvis does, and she's slightly smaller, but she also seems a bit fatter than she did the last time I saw her. Maybe she's been getting some extra paneer.

Krishnan and Mom appear at the door, and I try to be patient while they do their boring grown-up greetings and air-kisses. Just when I think I'm going to explode if someone doesn't tell me what the surprise is *right now*, Krishnan says, "So, should we tell Ella the exciting news?"

"Sure." Anjali beams at me—her smile is so similar to Krishnan's—and then she beams at Minerva. "Ella, Minerva's pregnant, and Elvis is the dad! The puppies are due in three weeks."

I smile so hard I feel like my face might split down the middle. "Oh my god oh my god oh my god!" I squeal. "This is *amazing*! I thought she looked kind of pudgy—sorry, Minerva, no offense. How many puppies are there going to be?"

"The vet thought she felt five. And when they're born"—Anjali and Krishnan and my mom share another one of those significant looks, drawing out the suspense—"I'd love to give one of them to you, if you think you might be interested."

So much joy fills me up so quickly that I can't even speak right away—it feels like there are eight hundred helium balloons pressing on the inside of my chest. Then my words wriggle their way loose, and they come tumbling out all at once, tripping and falling and landing on top of one another. "Oh my god, *yes*, I am *so, so* interested! *Thank* you! Thank you *so much*. I've never had a puppy of my own before, or any dog of my own at all, actually, but I've been watching what Krishnan does with Elvis really closely, and I've been practicing super hard with him myself, and I know I could be *such* a good owner! And if you guys will help me, I think I could totally train a puppy to be a show dog! This is going to be the *best ever*." I try to hug Krishnan and Anjali and Mom all at once, and Minerva starts leaping around us and barking with excitement, and everyone stumbles off-balance and laughs, and it's pretty much the best moment of my entire life.

"We know you're going to be a great owner," Krishnan says. "You're the most responsible kid I've ever met. This puppy is going to be so safe and happy in your capable hands."

"*Thank you,*" I say, and I bury my face in his chest and breathe in his mint-and-detergent smell. I can't believe there was ever a time when I worried about my mom marrying him.

"Can we do a Harry Potter theme for the names?" I ask. "Their names should have something to do with Minerva's name if we want them to be good show dogs, right? And I know Minerva's a Greek goddess, but it's also Professor McGonagall's first name, so maybe—"

Anjali laughs. "Let's see what they look like when they're born, okay? There's plenty of time to think of names. Are you hungry? Dinner's ready."

"Definitely," I say. "I have to do something for one second, and then I'll be right there."

"Okay," Anjali says, and she and Mom and Krishnan head down the hall to the kitchen.

I grab Minerva's collar to keep her there with me, and when I'm sure the adults are gone, I crouch down and press my face against her belly. She shifts around and sniffs my head for a minute, but then she calms down and lets me do it.

"Hi, puppy," I whisper. "I'm your future owner, Ella, and we're going to be best friends and go on all kinds of adventures together, and it's going to be *amazing*. I already know you're the cutest dog in the world, and I can't wait to meet you." I feel kind of ridiculous, but Mom said she used to talk to me before I was born so I'd know her voice when I came out, so I don't see why the same thing wouldn't work with a puppy. Visions of doing dog shows with her dance through my head; if she gets used to my voice *now*, we're already going to have crazy dog-owner mind-meld by the time she's born. I'm going to know what every single tail wag means. I'm going to love this puppy so, so much, and she's going to love me back unconditionally *and* be a champion, and it's hard to imagine anything better than that.

Dinner is ridiculously delicious, and I stuff myself full of saag paneer and naan and pakoras until I feel like I'm about to explode. Then Anjali brings out a stack of board games, and we settle on Pictionary, Mom and Krishnan versus Anjali and me. My aunt and I are both perfectly decent at drawing, but we don't stand a chance against my mom and stepdad. Maybe it's because I was thinking about mind-melds earlier, but I start to notice what amazing mind-meld the two of them have—they're almost always able to guess what the other one's drawing when it still looks like a blob to me. There's one turn where Mom draws a circle—a plain *circle*—and Krishnan correctly guesses "avocado." And it's not only in the game, either. They're constantly refilling each other's drinks before the other one asks or passing the right thing when all the other one says is "Honey, can I have the—." I know it's cliché to say that a couple is so close that they finish each other's sentences, but Mom and Krishnan literally do it all the time. I try to remember if Mom ever did that with Dad, but all I come up with is a memory of her snapping, "I can't read your mind, David!" when he was annoyed with her for not doing something.

The mind-meld is special, and it can't happen with just anyone. But Mom found it with Krishnan, and I sometimes have it with my best friends, and I'm definitely going to have it with my new puppy. Everyone deserves to know how that feels, and I'm more determined now than ever to find it for my dad. There has to be someone out there who's broadcasting the right wavelengths that'll make his antennas tingle.

When we get home, I have one extra spoonful of the leftover food Anjali wrapped up for me—okay, maybe four—and then I bring my laptop into bed and cannonball into my dad's Head Over Heels inbox. There are seventy-four women to sort through, which would normally seem overwhelming, but tonight I'm so optimistic that it barely feels like work.

It's much easier to narrow down the women this time, since I need someone with a career that'll allow me easy access to her. I'm immediately able to eliminate an anesthesiologist, an engineer, a wedding planner, three computer programmers, and an architect, even though a couple of them look pretty good. There's a photographer who seems promising—I could pretend I want to have my portrait taken as a gift for my dad's birthday—but then I discover she's a Yankees fan. There aren't any tutors or waitresses, like Miriam suggested.

But just when I'm starting to get frustrated, I find Sirsasana77. She's a yoga teacher who lives in the next town over and is taking night classes to get her massage therapy license. She loves to cook, she's obsessed with the same TV shows as my dad, and her profile says she definitely wants kids. There's even a photo of her with a dog. I don't believe in fate, but I can't help it—there's a part of me that feels like this is meant to be.

Best of all, I recognize the studio, Lotus Yoga, that appears in the background of one of her photos—I'm pretty sure it's in the same strip mall as my mom's favorite Thai restaurant. I find the About Us page on Lotus's website, and bingo, there's the woman's picture in the list of teachers next to the name *Beth Jackson*.

I click on the studio's class schedule for the coming week, and I start plotting.

— 12 —

I put my plan into action on Wednesday after school. As soon as the bell rings, I text Dad to tell him I'm going for a bike ride and will be home by dinner, and then I pedal down the bike path to Beth's yoga studio. I pull over a few doors down, lean against the wall between a hair salon and the Thai restaurant, and run through the procedure in my head step-by-step until I feel calm. I smear on a dab of lucky watermelon lip gloss, and then I'm ready.

A few minutes later the door of the studio opens and a bunch of Spandex-wrapped people come out carrying mats. I study each face, but none of them is Beth. One by one they get into their cars and pull out of the parking lot, and then nothing happens for what seems like a really long time. I start to worry that I got the schedule wrong, or that Beth is out sick today, or that she doesn't even work here anymore.

But then the studio door opens again, and there she is.

She's wearing a white hoodie and shiny leggings patterned with green fish scales; I would totally wear those to ballet class if Ms. Caroline didn't insist on a strict dress code. The yoga mat sticking out of her bag is my favorite shade of purple, and she's smiling as she walks, even though she's by herself. In her profile picture, she had tiny microbraids—Jordan got those once, and she told me she had to spend the *entire day* at the salon. But Beth's wearing her hair natural now, and her short, tight curls catch the late afternoon sunlight and glow.

I test to make sure my helmet is secure, and then I push off and ride toward her.

Beth's car is at the opposite end of the lot, right next to a little island of grass and fallen leaves. As she unlocks her door, I ride behind her, then turn abruptly so that my front wheel smacks into the curb. The bike lurches sideways, and I topple over onto the grass like I planned, absorbing most of the impact with my right hip and shoulder. Cold, muddy water instantly soaks through my jeans and sweatshirt, and the bike falls on top of me, pedals still spinning. It's not exactly comfortable, but sometimes you have to make sacrifices for love.

"Owwww," I groan.

Beth is beside me in an instant, extracting the bike from my tangled limbs. "Oh my god, what happened?" she asks. She has a pretty voice, low and musical—I can totally see how it would be soothing in a yoga class. "Are you okay?"

Am I okay? I roll over and take stock. I'm definitely going to have bruises on my hip and shoulder, but that's nothing I can't handle. Nothing feels twisted or broken, so I should be able to go to dance class tomorrow with no problem. My ankle stings where the curb scraped it, and when I look down, I see that it's bleeding exactly the right amount to look pathetic. I couldn't have fallen better if I'd tried.

"I think so," I say. "My ankle's a little scraped up, but otherwise—"

Beth pushes up the leg of my jeans, and her eyes get all soft. "You're bleeding, you poor thing. Is your mom or dad around here somewhere?"

"No, I'm out for a ride by myself."

"There's a first aid kit in the yoga studio—that's where I work. Do you want to come inside for a second? I can clean this up and give you some Band-Aids. Or I can bring them out here if that makes you more comfortable."

I sit up and rub my elbow—yup, I'm going to have a bruise there too. "I can come in. Thanks."

"I'm Beth, by the way."

Oh, I know, I want to say, but instead I tell her, "I'm Ella."

"That's one of my favorite names," Beth says. "It's nice to meet you. All right, let's get you on your feet."

She squats down, loops my arm around her shoulder, and before I know it, I'm standing—she is *ridiculously* strong. Her back muscles are rock-hard, and I wonder if all of this came from doing yoga. "Do you think you can walk?" she asks.

"Yeah. I'm not sure I can ride all the way home, though. I should probably ask my dad to come get me."

"Of course," she says. "We'll give him a call."

Beth steers me toward the studio, wheeling my bike along with her other hand. The right side of my body is completely coated with muddy leaves, and they fall off like a trail of breadcrumbs as we walk. They make me look even more bedraggled, so I don't brush them off.

Beth parks my bike next to the door and leads me inside, where I'm hit with the smell of incense mixed with fresh sweat; it should be disgusting, but somehow it isn't. I follow her down the hall to a tiny office, which has some filing cabinets, a desk covered in papers and an old computer, a bunch of random clothes lying around, and a dead plant in the corner. There's a yellow skateboard propped against the far wall. I expected something much more Zen.

"Sorry about the mess," Beth says like she's reading my mind. "It's not a very healing space, is it?"

"It's fine," I say. "I don't need to be healed, really. I just need a Band-Aid."

Beth opens a drawer in one of the filing cabinets and digs around for a second, then holds up a white plastic box with a red cross on the front. "Aha! Here we go. Have a seat, and we'll get you patched up."

I do what she says, and within seconds she's got my jeans rolled up and is dabbing at my ankle with a piece of gauze soaked in alcohol. It stings, but I love how gentle and competent she is. When I wince, she apologizes, then starts talking to distract me. "Ever tried yoga before?"

"I did once," I say. "Someone came to my ballet class. It was . . . okay?"

Beth laughs, and it makes her whole face brighten. Her teeth are super straight and blindingly white. "Not really your thing?"

"No, I mean, it was fine. I just prefer doing choreography."

"That's fair. But once you can do complicated yoga sequences, it actually starts to feel similar to choreography. One movement flows right into another. You might really like it."

"Hmm. Maybe I should try it again."

"Definitely," she says. "If everyone did yoga, the world would be such a happier, healthier place. I teach a class for kids on Saturday mornings—you should come check it out. How old are you, about twelve?"

"Yeah," I say. "Good guess."

Beth smiles. "I've got a niece your age."

Oh man, this woman is even better than I expected. "Really? Does she come to your class?"

Beth sighs. "No, she flat-out refuses to try it—she's more into stuff like martial arts. I'll get her here one day, though. I think she could really benefit from yoga. It would chill her out."

For a second I get lost in a fantasy of spending weekend afternoons hiking and going to movies and grilling steaks in the backyard with my dad and Beth and her awesome niece, who would obviously become my fourth best friend. If she does martial arts, she and Jordan would probably get along great. Maybe once I knew her better, she could start coming to sleepovers and EVGAPs and come see me compete in dog shows and—

"All right," Beth says, and I come back to earth to see that she's covered my scrape with two Band-Aids patterned with butterflies. "One more thing." She grabs her purse, flips open the front pocket, and pulls out a small clear crystal on a string, which she starts twirling back and forth above my ankle.

"Um," I say, "what are you doing?"

"It helps absorb bad energy," Beth says. "You'll be good as new in no time."

The spinning crystal is kind of hypnotic, but my ankle definitely doesn't feel any different. "Okaaay?" I say, trying not to sound too weirded out.

Beth laughs. "Well, it can't hurt, right?" She finishes up with the crystal and puts it away. "Are you sore anywhere else?"

I tell her the rest of me is all right, just bruised, but Beth helps me out of my muddy hoodie and insists on checking my shoulder and elbow joints. "Yeah, I think you're fine," she says. She shakes out my sweatshirt over the trash can, but even after all the leaves fall off, it's still pretty gross. "You can't wear this home. Here, I've got something you can borrow." She pulls a deep pink sweater out of her cavernous purse and holds it out to me.

"I'll get it dirty, though," I say. "My jeans are all muddy."

"That's okay. It'll wash out. You can drop it off here sometime next week." She dangles the sweater in front of me. "C'mon, it's really fine. It's too cold for you to wear a tank top."

I take the sweater and pull it on. It's warm and soft, and I like the way it smells like incense and coconut. "Thanks," I say.

"No problem. That color looks nice on you. I think you're a summer." I have no idea what that means, but before I can ask, she says, "Want to give your dad a call?"

I nod and pull out my phone, and it only rings twice before he picks up. "Ella?" he says, an edge of concern in his voice. "Where are you?"

"So, I'm totally fine, and you don't need to freak out," I say. "But I actually fell off my bike, and I need you to come get me."

"Oh no! Are you okay, sweetheart? Were you wearing your helmet?"

"Yeah, I was," I say. "It's not a big deal, I promise. I bumped into a curb in a parking lot and tipped over onto the island. But I'm all muddy and covered in leaves and I have a scrape on my ankle, and I just don't want to ride home like this."

"Of course not," Dad says. "I'll be right there. Where are you?"

"I was in front of this yoga studio when I fell—Lotus Yoga? This really nice teacher brought me inside and gave me some Band-Aids. Her name is Beth."

"Is she there? Can you put her on?"

"Sure! One sec." Before I hand the phone over, I rub the screen on my non-muddy thigh I hate touching phone screens that I have other people's face oil on them, and I want to show Beth how considerate I am. "My dad wants to talk to you," I say.

She takes the phone and breaks into a big smile as she talks, even though my dad can't see her. "Hi there, Ella's dad! This is Beth. She's absolutely fine." She's using this really happy, calm voice—man, how amazing would it be to have her around to pep him up *all the time*?

"We're at Lotus Yoga," Beth says. "It's in the strip mall on Sycamore, right near where it crosses the bike path." She's quiet for a minute. "Of course I'll wait with her. We'll see you soon!"

She hangs up and hands the phone back to me. "He'll be here

in five minutes. Should we wait outside?" I nod and follow her out of the office.

My dad arrives four minutes later—he must've been speeding. He pulls up right in front of the studio, hops out of the car, and pulls me into a tight hug. "I'm so glad you're okay," he says. "You scared me, Ellabee."

"I'm fine, I promise," I try to say, but it comes out muffled because my face is smooshed into his shirt. I pull back. "This is Beth. She did an awesome job of bandaging my ankle."

Beth sticks out her hand. "Good to meet you, Mr.—"

"Please, call me David," my dad says. "Thank you so much for taking care of Ella. You have no idea how much I appreciate knowing someone was here to help her." He takes her hand in both of his and sort of holds it instead of shaking it; I've never seen him do that before. In my head, I hear Daphne Langoria whisper, "Are those *sparks* I see flying around?"

"It was no problem at all," Beth says. "She's a great kid."

"She is, isn't she?" Dad beams, and I realize I've been going about this girlfriend-finding mission all wrong. I've been looking for people who shared interests with Dad when all I really needed was someone who would do the one thing Dad cares about most: be super nice to *me*.

"I checked her out for sprains and breaks," Beth says. "I'm not a doctor or anything, but I'm training to be a massage therapist, so I know a lot about bodies, and everything looks good to me. She'll have a few bruises tomorrow, but they should feel better if you put some arnica on them."

Dad looks bewildered. "Some . . . what?"

"Arnica? It's a homeopathic remedy for soreness and stiffness. Sorry, this is random, but have we met before? You look so familiar."

"No, I don't think so," my dad says.

It didn't even occur to me that Beth would recognize my dad from Head Over Heels, but I definitely have to stop this train of thought before it goes any further. "Thanks again for the sweater," I say. "Here, give us your number, and I'll text you to figure out a time I can return it."

"Sure," Beth says. She pulls a business card out of her bag and holds it out to Dad, and I snatch it and tuck it into my pocket. "You could always come to one of my classes and bring it then. Do you do yoga, David?"

"Ha," Dad says. "I'm not exactly what you'd call coordinated." He's right, which is really too bad; I read online that exercise is great for depression because it makes your brain release happy chemicals. But then Dad reaches up and starts rubbing the bald part of his head, which makes *my* brain release all kinds of happy chemicals— he's obviously embarrassed about looking unathletic in front of Beth, which means he cares what she thinks. Love is probably better at making people happy than yoga, anyway.

Beth smiles, showing off her Colgate-commercial teeth. "Well, there's a beginners class on Tuesday at seven if you're ever interested in giving it a try. You two could come together. It doesn't matter if you're not very stretchy yet; I could teach you some modifications. I just like to bring inner peace to the world, one person at a time."

"All right, I'll keep that in mind," says Dad, and I want to do a happy dance right there on the sidewalk. There's no way Dad's actually interested in trying a yoga class, so he must want an excuse to see Beth again, and she really seems to like him too. Miriam is a total genius.

My brain is spinning like a tornado now. I'll create a fake e-mail address, write to Dad pretending to be Beth, and ask him out. Later on, once they're together and she writes to him from her real e-mail, I can say the first one was her work address. Then I'll text Beth from my phone pretending to be my dad and ask *her* out. Both of them will show up at the same place, each thinking the other one did the inviting. But unlike last time with Linda, both of them will actually *know* they're supposed to be on a date.

Don't worry, Dad, I want to say. *I'll get you an awesome girlfriend before you know it, and you won't even have to wear Spandex shorts.*

E-mails between "Beth" (me) and Dad:

To: David Cohen<davidcohen@smgadvertising.com>

From: LotusYogaBeth<lotusyogabeth@gmail.com>

Hi there, David!

I know this may seem like it's coming out of nowhere, but after I met you yesterday, I looked you up on your company's website! (Ella told me where you worked.) I hope you don't mind. It's just that I never meet guys who seem so funny and sensitive and concerned about their kids, and I'd really love to get to know you better! Ella told me you're divorced, so I thought it was possible you might be single. If you'd like to go out sometime, maybe we could meet up for dinner next week?

Sincerely,

Beth

To: LotusYogaBeth<lotusyogabeth@gmail.com>

From: David Cohen<davidcohen@smgadvertising.com>

Dear Beth,

Nice to hear from you. First of all, thank you again for taking such great care of Ella the other day. Knowing there are kind people like you out there who will help her if she needs it makes letting her do things on her own a tiny bit easier for this overprotective dad.

I was surprised to get your message, but not unpleasantly so! Yes, I've been divorced for a couple of years now. I've been holding off on dating mainly because I thought it would be too hard on

Ella, but she actually came to me the other day out of the blue and *encouraged* me to start dating again. Not really sure where that came from, but maybe I should take it as a sign. So . . . yes, why not. How about Tuesday at 7 p.m. at Supernova on Sumac St.? Here's to my clumsy kid bringing us together!

David

Texts between "Dad" (me) and Beth:

Today, 7:58 p.m.

> **Me:** Hey, this is Ella's dad, David! I wanted to say thanks again for taking such good care of Ella the other day!
>
> **Beth (Yoga):** Hey! No problem at all.
>
> **Me:** I also wanted to ask you something.
>
> **Me:** I know this maybe seems like it's coming out of nowhere, but . . . any chance you'd like to hang out with me sometime? You seem like a really cool person.
>
> **Me:** Sorry if this is awkward or if you have a boyfriend. (Or a girlfriend.)
>
> **Beth (Yoga):** Haha, definitely surprising, but not awkward!
>
> **Beth (Yoga):** I'm not seeing anyone at the moment, actually.
>
> **Beth (Yoga):** So yeah, let's grab a drunk sometime soon?
>
> **Beth (Yoga):** A DRINK. Stupid autocorrect.
>
> **Me:** LOL. Awesome! How about Tuesday at 7 at Supernova on Sumac St.?
>
> **Beth (Yoga):** Sounds great! See you there!

— 13 —

I'm supposed to be at Mom's house the night of Dad's first date with Beth, but there's absolutely no way I'm missing their meet-up. My plan actually seems to be working—*finally*—and after the last two dating disasters, I can't wait to watch something go well.

This time I rule out spying on Dad from inside the restaurant; I am *not* spending another evening dodging elbows and knees under a table. But that doesn't mean someone *else* can't be my spy on the inside, as long as that someone is in disguise. Miriam has a piano lesson on Tuesday night, and Jordan's having dinner at her grandma's house, but Keiko is free. She also has easy access to costumes; her sister Yumi was obsessed with anime cosplay for awhile, and she left all her wigs behind when she went to college. Keiko promises to bring one for each of us so I can lurk outside the restaurant window without Dad and Beth noticing me.

On Tuesday night I tell my mom I'm going to Keiko's for

dinner, and Keiko tells her parents she's coming to my house. Then we convene at the Starbucks down the street from Supernova to get ready. Unfortunately, it turns out Yumi didn't have any normal-colored wigs—Keiko has brought a lavender bob, a long, curly, fire-engine-red one, and a bright blue one styled in pigtails with big pink bows. We pick the lavender for Keiko, since it's the most inconspicuous. The other two will make me so much more notice-able than usual that I decide to skip the wigs and just pull up the hood of my sweatshirt while I lurk.

I get out the eyebrow pencil I swiped from Mom and shade in my friend's thin brows so they look thick and bushy, then draw a mole on her cheek. Once Keiko puts on a trench coat she found in her basement, an American Heart Association baseball cap, and a pair of dark glasses, she's pretty much unrecognizable. I offer her the watermelon lip gloss, and we both dab a little bit on, but I don't think we'll even need it. Dad and Beth clearly like each other already, and I have a good feeling about tonight.

"You look perfect," I say. "Ready?"

"Ready," she says.

Keiko takes off first, and I stay at the Starbucks to wait for the all-clear signal—we don't want to risk my dad spotting me on his way into the restaurant. I spend eighteen nerve-racking minutes playing games on my phone, and then Keiko finally texts:

Keiko: The fisherman and the mermaid are in place
Keiko: Right side of the restaurant
Keiko: I'm 3 tables away. Tried to move to a closer table

but the server said it was reserved

Me: Can you hear them?

Keiko: Sort of . . . the music's kind of loud

Me: Who's facing the window?

Keiko: 🦐

Me: 👍 On the move. I'll call when I'm in place.

I hurry down the block. Supernova has huge windows facing the street, so I stop at the very edge of the building, which turns out to be right in front of Dad's parked car. I flatten myself against the brick and peek through the glass with just one eye; it's not the most comfortable position, but I can't let Beth spot me. She and Dad are right where Keiko said they'd be; there's another couple between us, so I don't have a perfect view of them, but it's good enough.

Keiko is three tables away, drinking a soda and typing on her phone, her head lowered so the lavender hair shields her face. She actually looks pretty ridiculous, but nobody seems to be staring. I dial her number, and she picks up right away. "Lighthouse, do you copy?"

"Loud and clear," I say. "How's everything going? Have the fisherman and the mermaid spotted you?"

"Nope," she says. "The hostess looked at me kind of weird when I showed up, but I told her I was waiting for my mom to get out of work and pick me up."

"Cool," I say. "So what happened when they got there? Did they shake hands? Or, like . . . kiss?" Even though I really want this date to go well, it's weird to think about them kissing.

"They hugged," Keiko says. "It was awkward—it was like they

couldn't figure out whose arm should go on top. But it was kind of cute. She's really pretty. I like her shirt."

"Me too. What have they talked about so far?"

"I'm only catching, like, every other sentence," Keiko says. "They're talking about how their days were. It sounds like Beth taught a yoga class where some lady went into labor?"

"Eww," I say. "Does my dad look totally squicked out?"

"A little," says Keiko.

"I hope she's not giving him too many details. He gets woozy just thinking about blood." What if my Dad faints on his very first date since the divorce? He'd probably never talk to a woman again.

Fortunately, a server with tattoos all up his arm arrives at their table and interrupts them. "Did you hear what they ordered?" I ask Keiko when he collects their menus and walks away. It's not like it matters, but it seems like some foods are more romantic than others.

"They said a bunch of foreign words. Maybe that was wine? I don't know. Then the fisherman asked the mermaid if she wanted to split some shrimp thing, and she said she's a vegan." Keiko pauses. "She said it kind of snootily, actually. Then she ordered salad. Something with arugula."

"Huh." Arugula doesn't seem romantic at all, but I guess maybe it is if you're vegan. I revise my daydream about grilling steaks with Beth and Dad. I wonder if she'd be upset if we ate meat in front of her; he and I are pretty huge carnivores. I really hope that's not going to be a problem.

"Oh no," Keiko says. "They turned the lights down, and now I can't see anything with these sunglasses on. Do you think I can take them off?"

Beth and Dad seem pretty absorbed in their conversation, and there's another couple sitting between them and Keiko now. Plus she's still got the wig and the hat and the weird eyebrows; my dad would have to be paying close attention to recognize her. "Yeah, it's probably fine," I say, even though I'd rather she play it safe. "Go for it."

My friend takes off the glasses and tucks them into the pocket of the coat. "Much better. Okay, the fisherman is asking the mermaid about her massage therapy classes. She's saying she goes to school at night. That's cool."

Beth is making big sweeping hand gestures as she talks; she wasn't doing that the other day at the yoga studio, and I wonder if it means she's nervous. If it does, is that a good sign or a bad sign? It could mean she cares what my dad thinks of her, which is definitely good, but it could also mean he's not putting her at ease, which is less

Beth flings her arm to the right, and her hand smacks directly into the server, who's about to put down their drinks. Keiko and I both gasp as two full glasses of red wine go flying, splashing all over the table and down the front of my dad's shirt. Since he's facing away from me, I can't tell exactly how much went on him, but judging by the way he leaps out of his seat like it's made of cockroaches, it must be kind of a lot. Beth claps her hand over her mouth.

"Noooooo," I moan. "Does he look mad?" I've worked so hard to get my dad out on this date; it *can't* be ruined in the first twenty minutes by something as dumb as a spilled drink.

"I don't think so," Keiko says. "He just looks really surprised. She keeps saying she's sorry over and over, and he keeps saying it's okay and that it's not her fault, even though it is."

Beth reaches out with her napkin, trying to blot my dad off, and he steps out of her reach—it doesn't bode well that he doesn't want her to touch him. "But is he saying it's okay like he *really* thinks it's okay, or like he has to *say* it's okay but actually he hates her?"

"Like it's really okay, I think?" Keiko says. "I don't know, I haven't spent that much time with your dad. Oh, okay, she offered him a stain stick, and he started laughing, so that's good. Now he's saying he's going to clean up in the bathroom. Oh wait. Oh no."

"What?" I say. "What's happening?"

"The bathroom's on the other side of me," Keiko whispers.

And then Dad's heading straight toward her. Instead of staying still so she won't attract his attention, Keiko lunges for the pocket of the trench coat to get her sunglasses. I know she's scrambling to hide her eyes, but the way she's flailing makes it impossible not to look at her, especially with the purple hair. "Keep going, keep going, keep going," I beg, but it doesn't do any good. My dad stops a few feet from her table, watching her with his head cocked to the left like a wine-soaked, confused bird.

"Keiko? Is that you?" I hear distantly.

My friend hesitates, and I can see her trying to figure out whether to lie. But there's really no use pretending—he already knows it's her. I guess she realizes that too, because she straightens up, brushes her lavender bangs out of her face, and smiles. "Hi, Mr. Cohen. What a coincidence running into you here."

My dad gestures to Keiko's head. "What's with the, umm . . ."

"Oh, we had play rehearsal today."

"I thought your school was doing *The Wizard of Oz* this fall," Dad says.

"Yeah, that's right," Keiko says. "This is my, um, munchkin costume. I didn't feel like carrying it home, so I thought I'd wear it. It helps me, like, get in the mindset of my character, you know?"

"Okay," Dad says. He sounds a little confused, but my friends are always saying and doing things he thinks are weird, so hopefully this won't seem too unusual. "Do you have a ride home?"

"Yup, my mom is coming to pick me up," Keiko says. "She should be here in a few minutes."

I wish she hadn't said that—now I only get to listen to a little more of the date instead of spying on the whole thing. But it does seem kind of odd for a twelve-year-old to be sitting alone in a cafe filled with adults at seven thirty on a school night, and the last thing we want is for my dad to get suspicious. I guess I can always keep lurking out here after Keiko "leaves." There wouldn't be any audio, but dating specialist Daphne Longoria can definitely read how a date is going based solely on body language, and maybe I'll be able to do it too. I've had some practice by now.

"Okay," Dad says. "Well. As you can see, my friend and I had an incident with the wine, so I'm going to go clean up."

"Perfect," Keiko says, obviously relieved that this interaction is over. "Have a good—"

"Wait a second," Dad says, suddenly excited. "I picked up my dry cleaning this morning. I have more shirts in my car." He turns back to Keiko and smiles. "You have a good night."

"Um, you too," she says.

And then my dad turns and heads toward the front door.

To go to his car.

Which is directly behind me.

I see Dad's words register on my friend's face at the exact same moment that I realize what's happening. "Oh no," she says. "Ella."

I don't even pause long enough to answer her. In one fluid motion, I hang up the call, shove my phone in my pocket, and run.

Today, 7:21 a.m.

Me: OMG you guys look at the text Beth sent my dad at 1:34 in the morning!!!!

Me: "Hey, I had a great time tonight! Even if I never get you into a yoga studio, I'd love to see you again sometime soon. Or I'd be happy to give you a private session, if you're too much of a wimp to wear Spandex in public. ;)"

Keiko: WINKY FACE!

Keiko: Aaaaaahhhhh I knew it, she likes him so much

Mir: !!!!!!

Keiko: I'm SO glad you got away before he went outside!

Me: OMG ME TOO. SO CLOSE.

Jordan: She wants to see him in Spandex, gross

Mir: Did you pass the message on to him?

Me: Yeah I e-mailed it

Me: AAAAAAH he wrote back already!!!!

Me: "I had a great time too. No yoga for me, I'm afraid, but I'm happy to scarf down more guac with you anytime. Maybe we should have our wine in sippy cups, though . . . ;)"

Keiko: WINKY FACE BACK!

Keiko: So he wasn't upset about the wine!

Me: So relieved

Keiko: When did they get guac tho? Must've been after we left

Jordan: 🥑

Me: Should I give her his real phone number?

Me: They don't need me to pass messages back and

forth anymore, right? I'm srsly just copying and pasting at this point

Mir: DO IT

Me: K. I'm gonna say he's switching phone companies and this number is getting shut off later today

Mir: Eeeeeeee so exciting! 😁😁😁

Jordan: Send us her profile!

Mir: YES YES YES I WANNA SEE

Me: K hold on, let me find it

Me: Guys

Me: It's not here

Keiko: It's not where?

Me: On the site!

Me: How could it not be here???? It was up last night!

Jordan: Maybe she made it private?

Keiko: Can you do that?

Jordan: Yeah, when my horrible aunt Libby does online dating she's always taking her profile down

Jordan: She'll be like OMG I found The One, I'm going off the site

Jordan: And then two weeks later it turns out The One has 17 ferrets or runs a cult out of his basement or something and she puts her profile back up

Keiko: She dated a guy with 17 FERRETS?

Jordan: I dunno I don't really listen

Me: You think Beth took her profile down bc she thinks my dad is The One?

Mir: That's totally it! Don't people say you're supposed to just KNOW when you meet the right person? Maybe that happened with them last night.

Keiko: They stared into each other's eyes over a bowl of guac and their souls connected . . .

Me: MAN I can't believe we didn't get to see that!!!!!

Me: But you guys.

Me: WE DID IT

Me: WE TOTALLY MADE TWO PEOPLE FALL IN LOVE

Me: WE ARE SO AWESOME

Jordan:

Mir:

Keiko: ♥ ♥ ♥

Jordan: No fair that Keiko got to see her and we didn't, tho

Me: If everything goes as planned you'll see her in Philly!!!

— 14 —

The Providence dog show doesn't have a juniors division, and after competing in two shows in a row—or trying to, anyway—it's weird to show up at the convention center in normal clothes. I wish I *were* going into the ring today, honestly; it makes me really nervous that I won't get another chance to practice in front of a judge before the National Dog Show. Nearly everyone else there will be used to winning, and I've never even *completed* a show successfully. It's hard to trust that practicing in the backyard will be enough, even though I've been training with Elvis a ton. On Friday I had Krishnan time how fast I could get Elvis into a perfect stack over and over until we managed to reduce how long it took by a full eight seconds. It's not like you get points for speed or anything, but the more seamlessly my dog and I work together, the more impressed the judge will be.

I usually stick with Mom and Krishnan all day at shows, running errands and helping with Elvis. But today they've agreed to let me go off on my own so I can collect data for my science fair project. Mom makes me promise to text every half hour, and Krishnan tells me when and where Elvis's ring time is so I can come cheer them on. It seems like it would be boring to watch twenty Welsh springer spaniels trot around in the same exact pattern, one after another, but now that I'm starting to see tiny differences in the ways people handle their dogs, it's actually pretty interesting. Plus I know how I feel every time my dad is absent at one of my performances or competitions, and I don't want anyone else to feel that kind of disappointment because of me.

I give Elvis a big kiss on the nose for luck, and his tail does this swishy diagonal wag that I'm pretty sure is the "I love my people" wag. Then I check my duffel bag to make sure I have all my scientific materials and the spreadsheet where I'll record each dog's information. The more dogs I test, the more accurate my results will be, and if all goes well, I bet I can get fifteen trials in before lunchtime. I tuck two pencils into my bun and head toward the other side of the grooming area, feeling very official.

The convention center is as chaotic as always; it's not even eight in the morning and two Pomeranian owners are already fighting over a pair of scissors. Two people wearing giant plush dog heads like sports mascots are trying to distribute flyers for a new brand of dog food, but it doesn't seem like they've practiced with the heads on, and they keep bumping into stuff and getting clotheslined by leashes. Stan's there with his smoothie cart, but today I just wave at him from across the aisle—given what happened last time, I'm going to steer clear of smoothies for a while. I see a really cute purple collar and leash with a paw-print pattern, and I make a mental note to come back after I've done my trials and buy it for my future puppy, who's supposed to be born in less than a week.

I want to do my first test with the chillest owner and dog I can find, and when I spot a middle-aged guy reading a fishing magazine as his basset hound lounges at his feet, I know I've found the perfect candidates. I walk right up, head held high—nobody trusts a timid scientist—stick out my hand for a shake, and explain my experiment.

When I'm done talking, he says, "You do whatever you need to do, darlin'." I don't love being called pet names by strangers, but I'm willing to put up with it this once, for science.

The guy introduces himself as Irving and his dog as Hoover. Irving puts the basset in his crate, and together we wrap black fabric around the sides so he won't get distracted. I set up Krishnan's little digital camera on top, pointing down. Before I show Hoover his favorite things, I need a control, or a test that shows how he acts when he's seeing something he doesn't care about, so the first thing I do is stand in front of him for ten seconds with my hands at my sides. He stares at me with his big mournful eyes, his tail perfectly still. Then Irving hands me one of his dog's favorite snacks, and Hoover's tail goes crazy when I hold it up, wagging so fast I'm afraid it'll be a blur on the video.

My phone buzzes in my pocket, and I pull it out—Mom gets really antsy when I don't answer her messages right away. But it turns out it's Keiko.

Keiko: How's the dog science?

Keiko: On the way to my cousin's house so I can test her cats. OMG it's so early.

I want to keep the times between my tests consistent, so I shove the phone back in my pocket. Keiko won't be upset if I ignore her for a minute.

Next I hold up Hoover's favorite toy, which is a stuffed bear in a bumblebee costume. Again, his tail goes completely insane. For the last test, I ask Irving to stand in front of Hoover, face in a neutral expression. I wasn't sure the dogs would react if I didn't have the owners do anything, but Hoover cooperates, swishing his tail back and forth in a distinctly slower wag. I'm so excited that the test has been a success that I want to jump up and down and pump my fists, but I keep all my joy inside and act very professional as I fill out my spreadsheet, gather up my materials, and thank Irving.

My phone buzzes again, and I pause near a booth selling dog hair bows. There are so many texts that they don't even all fit on the screen. Keiko must be *really* bored in the car.

> **Keiko:** So mad my mom couldn't take me later
> **Keiko:** How do you get up so early for dog shows all the time?
> **Keiko:** I wish I could drink coffee but coffee is gross
> **Keiko:** Maybe it would be okay if I put a ton of sugar in it? Then it would be like a hot Frappuccino
> **Keiko:** Now I want . . .

A whole parade of Dalmatians goes by as I unlock my phone to answer, which is totally perfect—Keiko was obsessed with *101*

Dalmatians when we were little and can still recite most of the lines.
I snap a picture of them and send it to her in reply.

> **Me:** Trust me, I wouldn't get up this early either if my mom
> and Krishnan didn't make me. Hope these cute faces
> cheer you up!

I spot a Shih Tzu who looks like a pretty promising test
subject—I want to get dogs of all different sizes—and my phone
buzzes again as I'm heading across the aisle toward him.

> **Beth (Yoga):** ??????

I stop walking.

As I stare at the screen, this horrible chilled feeling sweeps
through my body, like all my organs have been replaced with that
blue gel that's inside cold packs. Moving so slowly and deliberately
that it's almost like a dance, I take my duffel bag off my shoulder and
set it on the floor. My hands shake as I open my texts and frantically
scan the window where I pasted the Dalmatians, hoping and praying
that I'm wrong about what I just saw, what I just *did*.

I'm not wrong. The text box I have open isn't Keiko's.

Another text comes through as I gape at my screen in horror,
and then another.

> **Beth (Yoga):** What about your mom? Who's Krishnan?
> **Beth (Yoga):** Is this David? I thought you switched numbers?

And then the phone rings, and my screen shouts BETH (YOGA) in big, glowing letters.

When I was six, I accidentally mentioned my mom's surprise fortieth birthday party right in front of her. The expression that bloomed across my dad's face right before I realized my mistake is burned into my memory forever, and that's the image I see in my head right now.

What have you done? says that look.

I should never have trusted you to handle something so important.

Now you've ruined everything.

I turn off my phone, shove it into my pocket, and vow that I will put this out of my mind and concentrate on science, that magical place where you get to control every variable, then take all your messy data home and not show it to anyone until you've sorted it into neat, predictable patterns. Good scientists aren't supposed to be distracted by their emotions. But even as I work my way through trial after trial for the science fair, my knotted up stomach and sweaty hands and skipping heart won't let me forget that I've messed up the experiment that matters most.

For the rest of the day, that red voice mail icon lurks in the back of my mind, ready to explode into a million pieces the moment I touch it and destroy every single bit of progress I've made. If my dad never finds love and turns back into the person he used to be, I'll have no one to blame but myself.

— *15* —

Elvis doesn't win Best of Breed, which means we're free to leave early. And that means I can't avoid the Beth situation any longer.

As soon as we're in the car, I pull out my phone, and that evil little red circle glares at me accusingly, daring me to listen to my voice mail. For a minute I seriously consider throwing my phone out the window and trying to forget that my screw-up ever happened. But my dad genuinely seems to like Beth, and if she suddenly disappeared from his life, he'd probably get even more depressed than he already is, which is exactly the opposite of my goal. Plus, if I chuck my first phone into traffic after having it for only six months, there's no way my parents will buy me another one.

Mom and Krishnan are deeply involved in a boring conversation about some meal-delivery service and aren't paying attention to me, so I huddle up in the corner of the back seat, take some deep breaths, and press play.

"Hey, David!" says Beth's cheerful voice. "I'm so confused—I thought you said your old number was being shut off, but then I got a weird text from it, so maybe you are still using it? But you responded to me from your other number yesterday, and I'm not sure why you'd send me a picture of dogs? Maybe the number got reassigned to someone else . . . but I'm not sure why *that* person would send me a picture of dogs either. I tried calling, but the voice mail message is a robot. Anyway, call me back if this is still actually your number? I'm gonna try texting the other one again."

No. *No.* No, no, no, no, no.

I can't possibly deal with this alone, so I send my friends a message describing exactly how I screwed up and begging for help. All of them respond right away.

Keiko: OMG no, my Dalmatians messed up everything!

Jordan: You're gonna have to ghost her

Keiko: Arrrrrgggggghh this one was perfect tho!

Me: I can't do that! Ghosting is so mean!

Mir: That wouldn't work anyway . . . she has your dad's actual contact info.

Mir: She'll tell him about the weird text and the picture and he'll figure out it was from the dog show and know it was you.

Mir: She might've done that already.

I feel sicker than I did that time in fourth grade when Jordan dared me to eat an entire package of Oreos at once. But then something occurs to me.

Me: Wait, you guys. My dad is TERRIBLE about checking his phone on the weekends. He doesn't even respond to me most of the time.

Me: Maybe he hasn't seen Beth's messages yet?

Me: He probably would've called me if he'd figured out what I've been doing, right?

Keiko: Probably!

Jordan: Or maybe he's waiting till you get home to yell at you in person

Mir: No, I think he would've called. He probably doesn't know yet.

Mir: So you just have to get his phone before he does and delete the messages.

Dad's always leaving his phone lying around on counters and tables, and I'm pretty sure he still uses my birthday as his passcode. He'll be busy cooking for Italian Food Sunday when I get home, so maybe I'll be able to steal it and do what I need to do. My stomach, which was clenched tight as a walnut, relaxes the tiniest bit, and I feel able to uncurl my body.

After consulting with my friends, I text Beth:

Me: Hey, who is this?

Beth (Yoga): It's Beth

Me: From the yoga studio?

Beth (Yoga): Yeah. Who's this?

Me: It's Ella. You helped me when I crashed my bike?

Beth (Yoga): Oh hi!

Me: Sorry about texting you that dog picture

Me: I was trying to send it to my friend Bethany and I must've tapped the wrong name

Me: My dad gave me his old phone and I forgot to delete the contacts

Beth (Yoga): Oh, that makes sense! I was so confused. :)

Me: Ha, I bet

Me: You said you were gonna text my dad at his new number . . . did he answer?

Beth: Not yet

Me: When you do talk to him would you mind not mentioning the picture? He didn't want to give me a phone in the first place and I don't want him to take it back cause he thinks I'm not being responsible or whatever

Beth (Yoga): No problem, it'll be our secret.

Me: Thanks!

Me: Hey, why were you calling my dad anyway?

Beth (Yoga): He texted to thank me for helping you and we kinda became friends

Me: Oh cool ok! 😊😊😊

I slump against the window and take some deep breaths. So far so good. As long as Dad doesn't look at his phone in the next forty-five minutes, I should be in the clear.

When Krishnan pulls into Dad's driveway, I leap out of the car like the back seat is full of scorpions. I grab my backpack and my dance bag and run toward the house as I shout, "Love you, bye!" and blow a kiss over my shoulder. I fling open the door, kick my shoes off, and head straight for the kitchen, scanning the coffee table and the couch and the dining room table on my way—no phone. I peer around the kitchen door. Dad's chopping veggies, and I skim the counters around him, but all I see are salad ingredients, empty jars of sauce, and half a ball of mozzarella. The kitchen table's set for dinner, but there's no phone there either. Where *is* it?

"Hey!" I say, trying to sound not panicked.

"Hi, kiddo!" Dad puts down his knife and hugs me. His voice is breezy and normal, which is a relief—if he'd gotten Beth's messages, he'd probably be a little tense. I still have time to fix this. "How was your day?"

"Pretty good," I say as he lets me go. "I did a bunch of trials for my science fair project, and I think I'm starting to see some patterns in the tail wags. It smells really good in here. What are you making?"

"Chicken parm," he says. "I think it's about ready to come out. You hungry?"

"Starving," I say. "I'll go wash my hands."

I head into the hall at a normal speed, but once I'm out of Dad's sight, I race through the living room and up the stairs. I search the office first, but the phone isn't on the desk or the end table or in the filing cabinet or between the cushions of Dad's favorite reading chair. It's not on his bed or nightstand or dresser or the counter in his bathroom. It's not in the guest bath. I even check in my room, though there's no reason he would've come in here.

No phone anywhere. The only logical place left is his pocket.

And if it's right there within his reach, anything could happen at any time.

In a flash of inspiration, I pull out my own phone and dial his number as I run back downstairs—an incoming call will take up the whole screen, so he won't see Beth's messages. That boring marimba ring every adult has starts chiming from the kitchen as I make my way through the living room. "Ellabee?" my dad shouts. "Why are you calling me?"

"My phone was acting weird earlier," I say. "I wanted to see if it was working. I guess it's fine now."

He silences the ringer. "What was wrong with it? We just got you that phone. It shouldn't be acting up already."

I shrug. "I don't know. I was trying to call Keiko, and it wouldn't connect."

"There was probably bad reception in the convention center."

"Yeah, probably." And then Dad sets his phone down on the counter. If I take five steps to my left . . .

"Ready to eat?" he asks. I tell him yes, hoping he'll have to turn back around to serve me, but he's already got a full plate in his hand, and he holds it out. There's tons of extra sauce, the way I like it, and my mouth starts watering like crazy. I take it and move toward the table, eyes still on the phone. Maybe I could say my glass is dirty, and then I could come back over here to get a new one and—

My dad's phone chimes with a new text.

Before I've even had time to think it through, I throw myself between Dad and the phone. My plate hits the counter and slips out of my hands, and chicken and cheese and all that beautiful extra sauce goes flying. Only a tiny bit gets on my pants—the rest hits the dishwasher—but my plate shatters into a million pieces on the floor. Thank goodness I wasn't eating off the octopus one tonight.

"Oh no, I'm so sorry," I say.

Dad's eyes go wide with worry, and he forgets all about the phone. "Did you cut yourself?"

"No, I'm fine. Just clumsy. Sorry about the food and the plate."

"It doesn't matter as long as you're okay. There's plenty of food."

"I'll go get the broom," I say. "Let me—"

"No, no, no," Dad says. "You don't have shoes on. Don't move or you might step on something sharp. I'll be right back."

He hurries to the front closet, and the second he's gone, I lunge for the phone. I'm just able to reach it if I stand on tiptoe on my left foot and stretch my arm as far as it'll go. It takes me a minute to make my trembling fingers type the passcode right, and for a second I panic that he's changed it, but the phone finally unlocks on the third try, right as I hear my dad close the closet door. There are four long texts from Beth, but I don't have time to read them. I write back "This is the correct number!" and then, with a few swipes and taps, I make the last few messages disappear.

And I'm safe.

Every single one of my muscles relaxes at once, and I want to melt onto the floor in a puddle of relief. But there's already a puddle of tomato sauce down there, so I don't.

"All right," Dad says as he comes back in, wielding the broom and dustpan. "Let's—What are you doing with my phone?"

"Nothing," I say. "I mean, nothing bad. I wanted to see who texted you."

His eyes widen, and a panicked look crosses his face. "Who was it?"

"Your dentist's office reminding you to make an appointment for a cleaning."

Dad's face relaxes. "Oh. Okay."

"Who did you *think* it was?" I ask. I'm so giddy and relieved that I managed to delete the messages that I can't stop myself from teasing him a little. "Someone *special?*"

"*No.* There's— No." Dad holds out his hand. "Can I have that back now, please?"

I hold it out of his reach and dance it around. "Why, Dad? Is there all kinds of *secret stuff* on here you don't want me to see?"

He sighs and leans on the broom. "I wasn't going to tell you this tonight . . . but I guess now's as good a time as any."

"Wait, what?" I ask. "What weren't you going to tell me?" My heart breaks into an excited gallop—is he really going to say what I think he's about to say? I definitely didn't picture this revelation happening while I was trapped on a tiny island of floor, surrounded by tomato sauce and broken plate shards, but I guess there's really no bad time for a person to say he's in love.

"Well." Dad takes a deep breath. "Remember how I promised that if I happened to meet someone awesome, I'd go on a date with her, even though I was afraid it might upset you?"

I'm not sure how my voice will sound if I open my mouth, so I just nod.

"As it turns out, I *did* meet someone pretty special. And it's actually all because of you."

It takes a second before I remember that even in Dad's version of reality, he met Beth because of me, and a flicker of fear must dance across my face before I can wipe it away. Dad's eyes get all soft and concerned. "Are you okay, Ellabee? Because if you're not—"

"No, I'm totally okay," I say. "That's great that you met someone! I'm really happy for you. But I didn't introduce you to anybody."

"Well, you did, in a way," he says, and then he rubs his bald spot. "Remember Beth? The woman who helped you when you fell off your bike?"

"Oh, her!" I pray my surprise looks genuine. "She was so nice. You're *dating* her? That's awesome, Dad!"

"Really?" He lets a little smile creep onto his face, which is super cute.

"Really! How many times have you been out?"

"Just twice," he says. "Tuesday and again on Friday. I was going to wait to tell you until it wasn't so new."

"But you had fun with her?"

"Yeah, I did." Dad peers into my face like he's trying to squint through my pupils and read the thoughts scrolling across my brain. "How do you feel about all this? Are you freaked out? Because if there's even a tiny part of you that feels like you don't want me to date after all, I'll call the whole thing off. No questions asked. You're entitled to your feelings, and it's up to me to respect them." He sounds a lot like Dr. Obasanjo, and I wonder if he asked her how to break this news to me.

"I'm not freaked out at all," I say. "I'm happy. Beth is really cool."

"She likes you a lot too. She keeps telling me what a great kid I have."

"We should have her over for dinner," I say. "Next Sunday! Can we? So I can get to know her?" By then, it'll only be two weeks till the National Dog Show; if I want them to go to it together, I need to plant the seeds right away.

"This seems kind of soon," he says. "We should probably wait and see if this is really going to become anything before—"

"Please, Dad?" I say. "She can have Italian food with us and see what an amazing cook you are. It'll be so great."

"Are you sure? Italian Food Sunday is kind our thing, isn't it? Maybe I should cook something else and we can have Italian food on Monday instead."

"You can make whatever you want," I say. "We can have Italian food twice. I just want to hang out with her."

Dad shrugs. "Okay. You're the boss. I'll ask her and let you know what she says." And then he crunches right over the broken plate and squishy globs of sauce and hugs me.

"Thank you for being so flexible and awesome, Ellabee," he says. "I'm really, really glad you're onboard with this. I want you to promise me that if you ever start to feel differently, you'll let me know right away so we can talk it out, okay?"

"I promise," I say into his chest. "But that's not going to happen. It's totally okay with me if things change a little bit."

— 16 —

People always accuse kids of being unable to sit still, but as we wait for Beth to ring our doorbell a week later, it's my dad who can't stop moving for two seconds. He paces back and forth and back and forth across the living room, tugging on his shirt cuffs, rubbing his bald spot, and picking invisible lint off his pants, which have such sharp creases that I'm pretty sure he actually ironed them. The clothes make me hopeful; he never wears anything around the house but his grass-stained jeans, and the fact that he's all dressed up when we're not even going out shows that he really cares what Beth thinks. But his constant fidgeting is making me seriously twitchy.

"You know it's not too late to change your mind about this," he says for the millionth time as he "straightens" a perfectly straight picture over the fireplace. "If you want her to leave, tug your ear three times like we planned, and I'll—"

"*Dad,*" I say. "It's *fine*. I'm the one who suggested we have her over in the first place, remember?"

"Right," he says. But he doesn't look convinced. Is *he* regretting inviting her over? I'll have to work extra hard to show him how much fun the three of us can have together.

The doorbell rings, and I spring off the couch to let Beth in. She's wearing this awesome black-and-white-patterned wrap dress and giant colorful earrings that clink every time she turns her head. It makes me feel totally underdressed in my sweatshirt and purple corduroys, but she looks really pretty, and when I glance over my shoulder at Dad, I'm relieved to see that he clearly thinks so too. She's carrying a bottle of wine in one hand and a poster tube in the other, and she doesn't seem nervous at all.

"Hi!" I say. "I'm so glad you could come!"

"Thank you for inviting me!" Beth pulls me in for a hug, and I'm enveloped in that same smell of incense and coconut that clung to the sweater I still need to return to her. "It's great to see you again. And I'm so relieved you're okay with your dad and me dating. I really wanted to tell you the other day when—"

"I'm *so* happy you're dating!" I say loudly before she mentions our text conversation about the Dalmatian picture. I try to give her a look like *You're not supposed to bring that up that, remember?* But she's already gazing past me into the living room, so she doesn't notice. "Come on in," I say instead.

Beth steps inside, and my dad gives her an adorably shy smile. "Hey," he says.

"Hi! I brought wine!" She hands him the bottle, and then the two of them do this awkward dance where Beth tries to give him a hug and he tries to give her a kiss on the cheek. When they separate, she holds out the poster tube and says, "Ella, I bought something for you too."

"Wow, thanks." I pop open the top, inch out the shiny paper inside, and unroll it on the living room rug. It's one of those inspirational posters that shows a mountain climber on a steep summit, silhouetted against a red-and-gold sunset. PERSEVERANCE, it says in big white letters. KEEP CLIMBING, AND SOMEDAY YOU'LL TOUCH THE SKY.

My first thought is how much Jordan would hate this poster; there are similar ones hanging outside our principal's office, and every time we walk by them, she makes noises that sound like a cat hacking up a hairball. My second thought is how concerned I am for the person in the picture—what is she planning to do after the sun sets? It's not like she can sleep up there, and climbing down in the dark would be super dangerous.

But saying any of that would be rude, so I thank Beth, and she beams at me. "I'll help you hang it up later," she says, and I smile and nod. The picture itself is legitimately pretty—maybe I can cut off the text part after she leaves.

Beth turns in a complete circle and takes in our couches and overstuffed bookshelves and fireplace. I love this room; Mom didn't take any of the living room furniture when she moved, so everything has looked basically the same since I was little. I think Beth's going to compliment Dad on what a cozy space it is, but instead she says, "I think the flow of chi in this room is blocked."

A crease appears between Dad's eyebrows. "The . . . what?"

"It's basic feng shui," Beth says, as if that explains everything. "See the way this couch is facing? It keeps the energy from passing through the space in a natural way. Picture the energy coming into your home as water flowing in through your front door. The goal is to guide that water around the room in a smooth curve so it won't run up against obstacles or leak out through the windows."

"Huh," says Dad. He looks totally confused.

"See, this window faces south. So to attract prosperity, that nice wooden chair should go there, in the southeast corner. Maybe with a small fountain? I have an extra one I can bring you. Here, help me move this couch."

"Um," Dad says. "Why don't we talk about this later? Dinner's almost ready." He doesn't sound upset, exactly, but he does sound pretty weirded out that someone who has been in our home for three minutes is trying to rearrange the furniture.

I like our stuff where it is, too, but more than that, I don't want this to affect Dad's feelings for Beth when she seems so cool in most other ways. I guess it's not *that* weird—she's obviously just trying to help us be more . . . energetic and prosperous or whatever. So I put on an enthusiastic voice and say, "It's cool that you know so much about, um, all this stuff. It's really interesting."

"Proper energy flow can make such a difference to a person's happiness," Beth says. "When I help you put up your poster, I'll take a look at your bedroom, too."

"Sure, maybe," I say. Fortunately, when I invite her into the kitchen in an attempt to change the subject, she follows me.

Dad and Beth open the wine she brought, and everything gets a lot better when they start talking about some environmental documentary they both want to see. The conversation flows easily now that they're not discussing couch placement, and I relax; there aren't any awkward silences at all, and they keep making each other laugh. Dad is way more

animated than usual, almost exactly the way he used to be when he and
Mom threw dinner parties when I was younger. A comforting warmth
radiates out from my chest as I sip my lemonade and watch them. The
inspirational poster and the energy weirdness don't matter as long as
Beth makes Dad happy, and it seems like she really could.

My phone buzzes in my pocket, and when I see the message on
my screen, I spring to my feet so quickly that my chair topples over.

Anjali: Minerva has been in labor for a little while! We're
expecting puppies within the hour!!!!

Dad gives me a startled look. "What's the matter? Are you okay?"
"Nothing! Yes! I mean . . . Elvis and Minerva's puppies are about
to be born!" My hands are trembling with excitement, and it takes a
few tries before I manage to type a reply:

Me: OMG OMG OMG!!!! KEEP ME UPDATED AND
SEND PICS THE SECOND THEY ARE BORN!!!!!!!!!!
🐕🐕🐕❤❤❤

"Who are Elvis and Minerva?" asks Beth.
"Elvis is my stepdad's dog, and Minerva is my aunt Anjali's dog—
well, my step-aunt, I guess? They're both Welsh springer spaniels—
Elvis and Minerva, not my aunt and my stepdad, obviously. Anyway!
They're having puppies, like, *right now*, and Anjali is giving me one of
them!" As I search through my phone for a picture of Elvis to show
her, it occurs to me that I probably shouldn't have mentioned Krishnan

in front of Dad while he's *on a date*. But when I glance over at him, his face doesn't look all pinched the way it usually does when I talk about my stepdad. Oh my god, having Beth here is helping already.

Beth takes the phone and peers at the screen. "Aww, he's so cute," she says. "I love dogs."

"Me too! So does Dad. Do you have one?"

"Not since I was a kid. We had a Havanese-Maltese mix named Oscar. He was the cutest ever."

Dad pulls a tray of his famous garlic bread out of the oven, arranges it on a plate, and places it in the center of the table alongside the pasta and salad. "Dinner's ready, if you ladies want to sit down," he says.

I love how he calls us "you ladies," and when Beth beams up at him and says, "Smells amazing, David," I feel like my heart is going to explode. This is exactly what I pictured when I imagined Dad being with someone.

Or . . . it's *almost* exactly what I pictured. The garlic bread doesn't taste the same without butter, and the pasta primavera isn't as good without the cheese or shrimp Dad usually puts in it. It's still tasty and everything, but I don't understand why anyone would choose to be vegan *on purpose*. I think about getting the parmesan out of the fridge for Dad and me, but maybe it would offend Beth and mess things up, so I keep quiet and eat my primavera plain.

I try to pay attention to the conversation and watch for flirtatious gestures between Dad and Beth—I know it's up to me to keep tonight on track. But after Anjali's text, it's pretty much impossible to concentrate on anything besides staring at the screen of my phone and waiting for it to light up again. It lies there silently for all of dinner, but the moment Dad starts clearing the dishes, a photo finally, *finally* comes through.

The puppy is the same size as the hand it's sitting in, which looks like Krishnan's. Its muzzle is mostly white, but there are two perfect auburn circles over its eyes, and its tiny floppy ears are pure auburn—perfect coloring for a show dog. Its nose is a soft pink, like the inside of a shell, and its eyes are closed. On the top of its head is a white splotch in the shape of a heart.

If you had asked me yesterday—or even half an hour ago—if I believed in love at first sight, I would've said no. But all of a sudden, I understand that sometimes it takes only a second to go from zero to loving someone with your entire heart.

Me: AAAAAAAAAAHHHHH SOOOOOOO CUUUUUUTE

Me: I LOVE IT SO MUCH

Me: IS IT A BOY OR A GIRL

Me: WHEN WILL IT OPEN ITS EYES

Me: CAN I HAVE THAT ONE

Me: AALFJNOWIRNGOINOEINKAJSKJFBOWBOEGBK

Anjali: LOL, it's a girl. It'll take her about two weeks to open her eyes.

Anjali: Don't you want to see the others before you pick which one you want? There are going to be four more.

Me: NOPE I DON'T CARE I WANT THAT ONE ♥ ♥ ♥ ♥ ♥ ♥ ♥

Anjali: LOL, okay. She's yours, babe. :)

She's *mine*.

"You guys," I say, breathless. "Look at my new puppy. Just . . . *look at her*." I'm buzzing with so much excitement that I feel like someone has plugged me into a faulty electrical socket, one that sends off random bursts of sparks and jolts of electricity.

Dad takes the phone, and his eyes get all melty when he looks at the picture. "Wow, she is *really* cute," he says.

"I know! I can't wait for you to meet her! Beth, look!" I hold up the phone, and Beth makes the appropriate *awwww* sounds, and then I snatch it back and text the picture to my friends. They respond right away with a landslide of exclamation points and dog emojis and hearts.

"I'm going to name her Hermione," I tell Beth and Dad, "and I'm going to train her to be a show dog. I'll start when she's really little, and by the time she's big enough to actually compete, she's going to totally trust me and do everything I want even if all I do is *think* it. It's going to be, like, this crazy owner-dog mind-meld. I mean, I love going into the ring with Elvis, but this is going to be a whole different thing on a *whole* different level."

"You compete in dog shows?" Beth asks. "That's really cool. Oh, is that where you were the other day when—"

"Yeah," I say, cutting her off before she can bring up the Dalmatian picture. "I've only done two so far, and neither of them was . . . um . . . very successful. But I'm actually competing at the National Dog Show in Philadelphia in two weeks."

"Oh wow, that's really exciting. That's the one they show on TV over Thanksgiving, right?"

"Yup. It actually tapes the week before that. They don't televise the juniors, though."

"That's a pretty big deal that you got in," Beth says. "Congratulations."

"I mean, I didn't exactly qualify for it," I say. "Usually you have to win first place at three shows to compete there as a junior, but they also do a lottery where you can be randomly selected to compete. It's so a couple of people who are new to handling can see what being in a big show is like. And I got super lucky and had my name chosen this year, so that's exciting! I've been practicing with Elvis *so* much, and I think he and I have really found our groove the last few weeks, so I know it's going to go way better this time."

"I'm sure it will." Beth turns to my dad. "You must be so proud of this kid."

"Always." Dad reaches over to squeeze my shoulder.

"I'd love to go to one of those big shows someday," Beth says. "I watch Westminster on TV every year."

My heart leaps into my throat and makes itself comfortable there. All the planning and scheming I've done has led up to this exact moment, and now that it's suddenly here, I don't feel ready. But Beth couldn't possibly have given me a better opening. I would be a fool not to take it.

"You should come!" I say with as much confidence as I can muster. "I'm sure you could drive down with my dad. Right, Dad?"

Beth's eyes get all big and shiny. "A road trip! That would be *so* much fun! We did tons of those when I was a kid, so I know all the good car games. I'd be happy to split the driving with you, if you wanted. And my college roommate and her wife live in Philly! We could make a night of it, go on a double date. What do you think?"

"Um," my dad says. He reaches up and rubs his bald spot so hard it's like he's polishing silverware, and then he opens his mouth again, but no words come out. He's totally trapped, and I feel kind of bad for him; if he wants to look good in front of his new girlfriend, he can't exactly tell her that he won't support his own daughter because he'd rather not be in the same room as his ex's new husband. But it's hard to feel too guilty when I'm doing all of this for his own good.

"That sounds *really* fun, Dad," I say. "You should definitely do it. I'll probably be hanging out with my friends after, so you guys will have the whole evening free." Under the table, I cross my fingers for luck, then cross my toes the best I can inside my socks.

And then Dad sighs and says the best two words I've ever heard: "Yeah, okay."

Dad is coming to my show.

I did it. *I did it!*

I honestly didn't think I could be any happier than I was when I got the picture of Hermione, but I'm so excited now that I feel like my brain is lighting up like the grand finale of a fireworks show. I don't even care anymore if Beth covers my room in inspirational posters or moves the bathtub into the living room; she is going to be so, *so* good for us. She and Dad have only been on three dates, and she's already making him so much happier and more relaxed and flexible and adventurous. Soon he'll stop wearing his grungy clothes and hanging around the house all the time, and he'll turn into his old self again, and everything will go back to how it used to be.

Just like I thought, all he needed was to start falling in love.

— 17 —

By now I've been to about a dozen dog shows, and I didn't think anything about them could surprise me anymore. But my eyes bug out of their sockets when we walk through the door of the National Dog Show. When Krishnan told me there were 175 breeds competing today and that some of the most popular ones, like the golden retrievers, had more than a hundred entries, I figured he had to be exaggerating. But there are so many people and dogs in these three giant halls that it actually seems possible.

Krishnan signs us in and gets instructions for where to set up our grooming table, and we walk through Hall A and into Hall B, past more vendor booths than I've ever seen in one place. There's a whole area full of JOG A DOG treadmills in various sizes, mostly in use, next to a huge banner advertising a dog masseuse who also does aromatherapy and crystal healing—Beth will totally love that. There are DogPedic memory foam beds and snack stalls selling horrifying things like cow kneecaps and buffalo knuckles. Even the dog bathrooms have fancy signs. Basically it's dog paradise. I can't wait to show it to Hermione next year. If all goes well, she will have been competing for six months by then and the two of us will have racked up enough wins that I'll qualify to enter the regular way.

I wish my friends were already here so we could giggle over all this stuff together, but they aren't arriving till noon; Mir's mom couldn't drive them down last night because of a work thing. Dad and Beth are supposed to show up around the same time. I'm nervous about how Dad will act toward Krishnan, but I remind myself that everything will be *so* much better now that Beth's in the picture. Today he'll see that being in the same room as my stepdad actually isn't so bad, and my whole life will finally get easier.

My ring time isn't until one, but Krishnan's is early, and by ten o'clock, he and Elvis have already been eliminated from the competition. A dog named George Harrison gets Best of Breed and will represent the Welsh springer spaniel group in the televised competition later on. Mom and I hug Krishnan when he comes out of the ring, but he doesn't really seem disappointed, which I can't understand for the life of me. I guess losing isn't such a big deal when you compete practically every weekend, but it's different for me. It would be horrible to fail at my very first big show in front of literally everyone I love.

A slow tentacle of fear starts creeping up from deep in my stomach, but I manage to push it back down. I could not possibly be more prepared for today than I am. My treat pouch is secured around my arm. I know to make extra sure Elvis and I both have empty bladders when we go into the ring. I bet there's not one single junior in this whole convention center who has practiced as much as I have, and there certainly aren't any others who've done *science experiments* to learn how to communicate with their dogs better. When I was watching Elvis in the ring, I tried to predict which tail wags he'd do while he waited for his exam and trotted around and gobbled treats from Krishnan's hand, and I was right a whole bunch of times, which means I'm finally learning to read him properly. I'm pretty sure everything is going to go perfectly.

So when Mom puts her hand on my back and asks, "You doing okay, Ellabella?" I give her a big, confident smile.

"Definitely," I say. "I hope you're ready to watch us win."

Mom's eyebrows crinkle together. "You're going to do great," she says. "But you know it doesn't matter whether you win or not, right? You've worked so hard for this, and we're all going be proud of you no matter what happens. The point of today is to have fun."

I'm about to tell her that *winning* is fun, but my phone buzzes in my pocket, so I pull it out.

Mir: There's an accident on the highway and we're moving suuuuuuper slowly

The nervous tentacle thrashes through my gut again, more forcefully this time. I start to type a message back asking if they'll still be here by one, but I'm not even done before another text pops up:

Dad: Hey Ellabee, we've hit some traffic and will be a little late.

"You're sure you're okay?" Mom asks. "You look pale."

I nod and stuff my phone back into my pocket. All my people will be here on time. The universe couldn't be so wildly unfair as to finally give me everything I need to make this moment perfect and then take it away again.

"I'm fine," I say. "Dad and Beth and my friends are all running late, but they'll get here."

"I'm sure they will," Mom says. "You want to go meet some dogs in the meantime?"

Obviously I want to meet some dogs.

While Krishnan catches up with some friends he hasn't seen in a long time, Mom and I wander around the convention center, making all the furry friends we can: an adorable Labrador named Adi; a pointer named Tucker; a terrier named Pepper; a pug named Zoloft, which my mom thinks is really funny for some reason. I'd love to test them all for my science fair project—I've only got data on twenty-one dogs, and I want a sample size of at least thirty. But when I mention to Mom that I wish I'd brought my crate cover and camera, she says, "Sweetheart, you don't have to be working every second. You have enough on your plate today. Try to relax, okay?"

An excited shout goes up from the next hall over, and when we follow the sound, we discover that the Diving Dogs competition is underway. One by one, dogs hurtle down a runway and leap into a massive inflatable pool with distance markers on the sides, chasing after the toys their handlers have thrown. My friends would *love* this. I text them a slow-motion video of a curly-coated retriever named Wally flying through the air, and they send back rows and rows of hearts and crying emojis and cars and those faces with the X-ed out eyes.

The next dog is my dad's favorite kind, a Samoyed, so I film that jump too and text it to him.

Dad: Amazing!
Me: ETA?
Dad: Maps app says 12:41.

Okay, okay. Everything is going to be fine. I tell Dad they should come straight to ring eight when they get here, and he responds with a thumbs-up.

A golden retriever named Waffle trots up the stairs and into position at the start of the runway. "So," my mom says in her *I'm trying hard to sound casual* voice. "Your dad's bringing a date today, huh?"

I nod. "Yeah. Her name is Beth. She's super nice."

Waffle barrels down the runway and lands with a gigantic splash that showers the people in the front row. "Twenty-two feet, eight inches!" says the announcer, and everyone claps.

"How long have they been dating?" Mom asks.

"Not very long. They've only been out four or five times, I think."

"That seems early to be introducing you."

"I actually met her first," I say. "Remember that time I fell off my bike a few weeks ago? She's the one who helped me and bandaged my ankle. Dad met her when he picked me up."

"Huh," Mom says. "Well, how do you feel about her coming here? Your dad dating is pretty new and different, and this is already a big day for you, and—"

"I'm fine with it," I say. "Seriously. I really like Beth. I invited her." I picture what Mom's face would do if I said *Actually, I tricked them into going out specifically so they'd come here together.*

"Oh," Mom says, obviously surprised. "Well, if you have any feelings about it and you want to talk about them, I'm always here. I know it took some work to get used to having Krishnan around."

"Are you mad that she's coming?" I ask. I've been so busy thinking about what might happen between my dad and my stepdad that it hadn't even occurred to me that this might be weird for Mom.

Her face softens. "No, baby. It's fine. I just . . . wasn't expecting it." She looks at her watch, and her Super Competent Mom expression slides back into place. "It's twelve thirty—you should probably start getting ready. I'll text Krishnan and have him take Elvis out for a pee break."

All of a sudden it seems like there are four hundred nervous tentacles slithering and sloshing around in my stomach, tangling around one another, but I say, "Cool. I'm going to run to the bathroom too."

"Do you want me to come with you?"

I roll my eyes. "No, Mom, I'm twelve. I can go to the bathroom by myself."

"Okay." She kisses my cheek. "I'll meet you at ring eight. You know where to go?"

I tell her yes, but as she walks off in the other direction, I suddenly do wish I had someone to go to the bathroom with. I pull out my phone and text Mir.

Me: Almost here?

Mir: Mom says ten minutes!

Me: Come straight to ring 8. You guys probably shouldn't say hi till after or Elvis will get really excited and I won't be able to calm him down.

Mir: ok! 😭 😭 😭

The bathroom floor is covered in dog hair and sequins, and there are signs posted above each sink that say ABSOLUTELY NO DOG-WASHING IN BATHROOMS. I pee and wash my hands, fix the flyaway wisps that have escaped from my bun, and apply my lucky watermelon lip gloss. My stomach is still twisting with nerves, but when I look at my reflection in the mirror, the girl who looks back at me—the girl the judge will see—looks confident and ready to win. Despite all odds, that girl made two people fall in love. A first-place ribbon isn't out of her reach.

I plant my hands on my hips in a power pose, and even though I know it's really dorky, I tell my reflection, "You've got this."

A middle-aged woman wearing a shirt that says I LIKE BIG MUTTS AND I CANNOT LIE pats me on the shoulder as she passes by on her way to a stall. "Yes, you do," she says. "Knock 'em dead, baby."

I get a little lost on the way to my ring, so Mom and Krishnan beat me there. After I rubber band my show number to my arm, I take Elvis's leash from my stepdad . . . and just like our very first show, he immediately starts tugging on it, shifting from foot to foot and whining. A girl a bit younger than me walks by with an adorable corgi, and Elvis lunges for him and tries to sniff his butt. The girl gives me a look like *Can't you control your dog?* and I feel my face turn bright red. I can put on a mask of confidence all I want, but Elvis knows what's underneath, and he's going to let everyone else know too. It seems so unfair that he can read my mind without even trying while I struggle so hard to understand what's going on inside his head.

I look around wildly, unsure what to do, and it suddenly feels like all the other kids are staring at me, laughing at me, even the tiny boy in the tiny suit who's carrying a tiny Chow Chow. He can't be more than six or seven, and even *he* doesn't think I belong here.

And the truth is, I don't. I didn't earn my spot in this show; almost everyone else won a bunch of other shows to qualify, and all I did was get randomly picked from a list of lottery applications. I'm a total fraud. What on earth made me think I could do this?

Elvis lunges after another dog, and I pull him back. "No, no, no," I whisper-scream, and my voice comes out high and hysterical. "You have to calm down, we practiced this, you *have* to—"

"Ella," Krishnan says, and he grips my shoulder. "Look at me."

I do, and staring into his warm brown eyes helps a little. "You can do this," he says firmly. "Elvis can sense if you're panicking, so you have to try to relax. You've practiced a million times, and you're going to be wonderful out there. Okay?"

"We love you so much," Mom says, and she gives me a hug. I breathe in the familiar smells of her citrusy perfume and shampoo, and it makes me feel the tiniest bit calmer. "We'll be sitting right there the whole time. Look at us if you get nervous."

"Okay," I say, but it comes out like a question.

And then I hear my name from across the ring, and when I look up, Miriam and her mom and Keiko and Jordan are all there on the other side, smiling and waving like crazy. Each of them is holding a giant, brightly colored sign covered in glitter and stickers. Miriam's says GO ELLA & ELVIS! Keiko's says YOU GOT THIS! Jordan's just says WOOF! in a speech bubble coming out of the mouth of something I assume is supposed to be a dog but looks more like a Sasquatch. Seeing my friends instantly makes me feel better, like a puzzle piece has snapped into place inside my brain. Now there's only one more missing piece, and he's on the way, and if he gets here in time, everything is going to be perfect after all.

As if I've summoned him, my phone buzzes in my pocket, and when I pull it out, the screen says *DAD*.

"Are you here?" I answer, breathless.

"We're at the front entrance," he says. "I'm so sorry we're late. There was an accident and we got stuck on the highway forever. Where should we go?"

"Ring eight," I say. "It's in Hall B. Hurry!"

"We'll be right there," he says. "Good luck, in case we're too late to hug you before you go on. Beth and I can't wait to see what you and Elvis can do."

"Thanks," I say, and just like that, all the tentacles in my stomach slink away, back into the slimy depths where they live. Everyone I love is here, which means everything is going to be okay now. I take a deep breath and let it out slowly, and the moment I do, it's like someone has flipped a switch inside Elvis—he stops tugging, sits down on the floor, and starts swishing his tail calmly back and forth. I am 99 percent sure it's the "I'm ready" wag.

"Well, look at that," Krishnan says. "Good job, Ella."

"Everything's going to be fine," I say, and for the first time today, I really believe it. Sure, maybe I did win the lottery instead of qualifying for my spot here. But that doesn't mean any of these kids are better than me. Everyone here had a first win at some point. Today is going to be mine.

— 18 —

The judge arrives, and the steward calls the kids who are ten
and under into the ring. I give the judge a once-over as the kids trot
past me with their dogs. She's older than my mom but younger than
my grandma, and she has a severe black bob that makes her look like
she should be playing the mean boss on a TV show about lawyers.
I'm surprised for a minute that there isn't a single sparkle on her
navy blazer, but then she moves, and I see that her skirt is somehow
plaid and covered in sequins at the same time. She's gentle and play-
ful with the dogs, but she doesn't smile at any of the kids. A couple
of them seem scared of her, but not me. She's clearly looking for
perfection, and that's what I'm going to give her.

Dad and Beth show up as the judge is examining the last dog,
and my whole body lets out a breath of relief, right down to my
fingernails. All the chairs are taken, but they manage to squeeze in
between two families who are standing near the corner of the ring—

when I do my down-and-back, I'll be running directly toward them. Beth smiles and waves when she sees me looking, and Dad shoots me the secret good luck hand signal I've been craving at the last few shows. I can't give him two thumbs-ups back because I'm holding Elvis's leash, but I do one angled one with my free hand. Having him here makes everything feel *right* in a way the other shows haven't. He even looks like his old self in this blue-and-yellow plaid shirt I remember from before the divorce, when he wore button-downs all the time and grungy T-shirts were only for yard work.

I put my hand on Elvis's head, and he gives it a sneaky lick. He's still doing the ready wag, and I feel like he's telling me he knows how important this is. He's going to do his very best to help me win.

The steward calls for the intermediate competitors, and I grip Elvis's leash tighter. "Let's go, buddy," I tell him, and he gets right up and walks next to me into the ring, his tail still swishing happily behind him.

The moment I walk through the gate, my world narrows to the size of the ring, and nothing outside of it matters. I feel so laser-focused that I don't even look at my family or my friends. Just knowing they're there and sending me love is enough.

Time seems to be moving both faster and slower than usual, stretching out and collapsing in on itself like taffy on one of those pulling machines. One minute I'm posing for a picture with the ten other kids in my group; I blink, and Elvis and I are waiting for his turn to be examined; I blink again, and I'm up at the front of the ring next to the judge without a clear idea of how I got there. I get Elvis into a perfect stack super fast thanks to all those hours we spent practicing with Krishnan, and when I dig a treat out of my pouch to hold above his nose, the judge nods at my arm and says, "Clever." My heart starts doing pirouettes—I don't think she's said anything personal to any of the other competitors. I am so, so in.

Elvis stands absolutely still as the judge feels his skull and checks his teeth and tests his ribs. He's alert and eager, as cooperative as he's been on our very best days of practice, and I can feel everything falling into place. The judge finishes her exam and scratches him behind the ears, and he leans into her lovingly and wags his tail like mad. "Good boy," she says. "Down and back, please."

Elvis and I glide across the ring together, working in perfect harmony like a single six-legged creature, execute a perfect turn at the end, and glide back. We are totally in the zone. When we reach the judge again, Elvis does what I'm pretty sure is the treat wag, so I feed him one, and when he locks eyes with me, I feel like we understand each other perfectly. There's no way the judge could help but notice.

"Right around, please," she says, and we float effortlessly around the ring. I'm absolutely as good as everyone else here. Elvis and I reach the end of the line and stop behind another girl and her bloodhound, and Elvis lies down on the floor and gazes up at me. I crouch down next to him and pet him, feed him treats, whisper to him about how amazing he is. I've finally given my very best performance, and my very best has almost always been good enough to get me what I want. I feel light and airy as I watch the judge examine the rest of the dogs, like I'm hovering just above my body. It's pretty obvious we're going to win.

And then the judge finishes working her way through the line and says, "Everyone all the way around together one more time, please." We follow the bloodhound in a perfect loop, and when everyone claps, my world expands a little bit. I see Krishnan snapping pictures, and my mom beaming with pride, and my friends holding up their signs, and my dad and Beth clapping and cheering, and the whole world feels perfect. Every obstacle and frustration I've been through in the last couple months has been worth it for this moment.

The judge calls certain dogs into the center of the ring: first the Border collie, then the Rottweiler, then some sort of small fuzzy terrier. It feels so inevitable that she'll call Elvis and me next that I'm not even nervous, and sure enough, she beckons us forward. I stand there at the end of the line, straight and tall. I can almost feel the ribbon in my hand.

And then the judge nods once, her helmet-hair swinging forward, and says, "Yes, that's how I want them. One, two, three, four."

But I must not be processing things correctly, because I swear she started counting from the wrong end of the line. *I'm* supposed to be number one, not the girl with the collie.

"What?" I say, but my ears are suddenly ringing, and I'm not totally sure I said it out loud.

Collie girl crouches down and hugs her dog, and then she makes her way down the line, hugging each of us. Her hair brushes my cheek as she embraces me and says, "Good job," but I'm so stunned that I don't even lift my arms to hug her back. I wait for someone to correct her, but instead the steward comes out, marks her number down in the judging book, and hands her a big purple first-place ribbon. And then there's a ribbon in my hand, too—a plain green one stamped with words in gold.

NATIONAL DOG SHOW

KENNEL CLUB OF PHILADELPHIA

JUNIOR DIVISION, INTERMEDIATE GROUP

FOURTH PLACE

"Congratulations," says the steward, and then I'm being herded out of the ring, past the line of teens waiting to compete. I have a vague feeling that I should be crying, but I'm so disconnected from myself that I can't even tell if there's a lump in my throat or not. Dad and Beth are closest, and they're next to me in a moment. Elvis leaps right up on Beth, who scratches his ears and says, "Oh my goodness, who's the *best* boy? Who's the most *handsome* boy?" and Dad pulls me into an enormous hug.

"Ellabee, that was *amazing*!" he says. "You had so much control over him!"

"It was just like at Westminster!" Beth says. "That was so impressive."

"Not impressive enough," I say into my dad's chest, and my voice comes out croaky and quiet. I guess I do have a lump in my throat after all.

Dad pulls away enough to hear me. "What'd you say?"

"I said it still wasn't *enough*." That familiar prickly feeling starts up in my sinuses, but I clamp right down on it like Elvis on a rawhide and forbid myself to cry. Even the little kids aren't crying.

"What do you—" Dad starts, but then Mom and Krishnan slip in next to us, and Elvis abandons Beth to jump up on my stepdad. "That was perfect, Ella," Krishnan says, rubbing the back of my shoulder. "I've never seen you handle him so well."

Mom pulls me into her arms and kisses me on the side of the head the moment Dad releases me. "I'm so proud of you," she says into my hair. "You were *wonderful.*" Then she turns to my dad. "Hi, David. Thanks for coming. And you must be Beth."

Dad and Beth awkwardly greet my mom, and Krishnan busies himself with petting Elvis. My dad crosses his arms tightly over his chest and doesn't speak to my stepdad, and Krishnan doesn't acknowledge him either, but there they both are, standing a few feet apart, and nobody's freaking out. I've proven that it *is* possible for them to be in the same place at the same time, and under any other circumstance, I'd be out-of-my-mind thrilled. But considering what happened in the ring, it's hard to even focus on the two of them or on a future past this moment.

"This isn't how things were supposed to go," I say, and my voice manages to crawl around the lump in my throat this time. "I did everything right. I was supposed to win."

"I'm sorry, sweetheart," Mom says. "You must be disappointed. But you know how subjective all of this is. The judges have such different tastes. Krishnan and Elvis had a great day earlier, and they didn't win either."

"But that's *different,*" I say. "This isn't about taste! That judge was looking for the best *dog,* and we can't control what Elvis looks like, but this one was judging *me*. I did everything I was supposed to do, and I tried to pay attention to exactly what Elvis was telling me, and I still— I didn't— I should've—"

And then my friends are there, piling on me like a bunch of puppies, poster board crinkling between us and shedding glitter all over my dress. "You were soooooo good," Miriam squeals. "Fourth place! That's amazing!"

"And it was only your second time *in* the ring!" Keiko says. "You're totally a natural. A dog show prodigy."

"I didn't—" I try to say, but Miriam starts talking again before I can get a full sentence out.

"Where's Beth?" she whispers. "Is she here? I want to see her."

"She's right—"

And then Jordan lets out an audible gasp.

"What's wrong?" asks Mir. "Are you okay?"

Jordan's staring wide-eyed at Beth, who's crouched on the floor next to Krishnan, scratching Elvis's belly. My friend looks equal parts scared and horrified, like she's watching a zombie eat someone's brain.

"Aunt Libby?" she says.

— *19* —

Beth looks up, and her face brightens. "Jordan! Oh my god, hi! What are you doing here?"

"I'm friends with Ella," Jordan snaps. "I'm allowed to be here."

Beth laughs. "Of course you are. I'm just surprised to see you." She looks back and forth between us with delighted wonder. "You two are friends? That's so crazy. Jordan, I was telling Ella a few days ago about how I had this awesome niece I thought she'd love. And I was right! I can't believe you already know each other! The universe is so amazing."

"Wait," I say. I'm feeling so many emotions at once that I'm having a hard time processing what's happening. "Wait. This is Beth. Why are you— Her name isn't—"

"It's Elizabeth," Beth says cheerfully, like none of this is weird at all. "You're both right. I go by Beth now, but I was Libby as a kid. My family still calls me that. Jordan's my oldest sister's daughter."

Oh *no*. We set my dad up with *horrible Aunt Libby*?

I'm so shocked that I can't even speak—I just stand there with my mouth gaping open like a dead fish. But Jordan starts laughing hysterically. "Oh. My. God," she gasps, bending over to catch her breath. "Are you *kidding* me right now? Of all the hundreds of profiles on Head Over Heels, *hers* was the one you—"

Miriam shushes Jordan and grabs her arm so hard that her fingers make little dents. "Hey, *stop*. You guys have to stop, or—"

"I didn't know," I say. "I swear it was an accident. Don't be mad—"

"I'm not *mad*! I'm just . . . oh man." Jordan wipes tears of laugher from her eyes. "If you'd shown us the profile, none of this would've—"

"*Stop,*" Miriam says.

"She tried to show it to us," Keiko says. "Beth took it down, remember?"

And that's when we notice that Mir's mom and my mom and Dad and Krishnan are all staring at us with matching confused creases between their eyebrows, and panic shows up to the feelings party in my chest. "Can we please talk about this over there?" I hiss. "Or, like, later? After we leave?"

"What's Head Over Heels?" Dad asks. He doesn't sound angry, exactly—just careful, like he's starting to realize the ice he's standing on might not be thick enough to hold him.

"Isn't that a dating site?" Miriam's mom asks.

"*What?*" my mom says. "Were you girls messing around on a dating site? I don't want you anywhere near those things. You're twelve! What were you thinking?"

"Oh my god, it wasn't for *us*!" I choke.

"Eww!" Miriam and Keiko say together.

Dad looks absolutely horrified. "What possible reason could you have for—" he starts. And then his expression changes, and he stares at me like he's never seen me before. The bottom drops out of my stomach.

"Ella," he says, his voice low and very, very calm, "please tell me this has nothing to do with the way you've been bugging me to start dating again."

It hurts to hear him call me plain old Ella. I can't remember the last time he called me anything but Ellabee.

Some tiny, frantic part of my brain is screaming that I can still salvage things if I can find the right words—the right lie—to make everyone believe that there's a reasonable explanation for what's happening. But I'm so overwhelmed that I can barely form a sentence.

"I'm so sorry," I manage. "I know I We— *I* shouldn't have done it that way. But I— I thought—"

"You thought what? That you had permission to force me into dating, even when I explicitly told you I wasn't interested?"

"Are you saying—" Krishnan starts, but Dad rounds on him and snaps, "Please stay out of this!"

"I didn't *force* you to date!" I say. "I couldn't have forced you if you didn't want—"

"I'm sorry, what is happening right now?" Mom asks. Her eyes are so wide I'm afraid they're going to pop right out of her face. "You signed your dad up for a *dating site*? Without his *permission*?"

I'm starting to feel a little dizzy, and when I blindly reach out for something to hold onto, my hand connects with a furry head. Elvis leans hard against my side, and I start to feel more grounded—I don't think I've ever been happier that he can instinctively read my emotions. When he gently licks my hand, the pure kindness of it almost makes me start crying, but I swallow hard and shove the tears back down.

Beth lays a gentle hand on my dad's arm. "Don't be mad at her, David. She was only trying to make you happy."

Dad whips around. "Did you *know* about this?"

"No! Of course not. But I'm just saying . . . does it actually matter how we met? People get set up all the time on purpose, and they have great relationships. How is this any different? The universe wanted us to be together, and now we are. Ella was only playing her part in the grand plan."

Dad stares at Beth like she's grown three heads and a glow-in-the-dark tail. "Let me get this straight. You're saying that you don't see any problem with my daughter impersonating me on the internet in order to pick up women?"

Beth shrugs, her face perfectly serene. "The road to happiness takes unexpected turns sometimes."

"I wasn't picking up women," I say desperately. "I was—"

"Ella, I need you to stop talking," Dad says. "I know that you're a child, and maybe you're not mature enough to understand how absolutely, ridiculously wrong this was. But *you*—" He turns on Beth. "*You* are old enough to know better."

"I understood what I was doing!" I say. "I'm not a baby!"

"Calm down, Ella," Krishnan says.

"Don't you tell her to calm down," Dad says. "This discussion does *not* involve you."

"Excuse me, but last time I checked, I'm Ella's parent too, and—"

"I'm not calming down!" I shout. My family and friends all stare at me—everyone in this entire convention center is probably staring at me right now—but I don't even care, and I wheel around to face Dad again. "*You're* the one who's acting immature, not me! *You're* the one who refused to come see me compete even though this was obviously super important to me because you can't be in the same room as Krishnan without getting all depressed!"

"*What?* That's not—" Dad starts, but I keep talking right over him.

"I don't need you guys to be besties or whatever! But he's going to be around whether you like it or not, and you can't stop showing up to support me because of him! When I asked you to come down to Philadelphia, you brushed me off like it wasn't important at all, like you didn't even care, and the only way I could think of to make you act like your old self was to trick you into falling in love again so you'd stop caring that Mom did!"

Everyone stares at me in silence, disbelief painted all over their faces, and then Mom says, "Oh my god, Ella," in this gentle voice, and suddenly all the embarrassment I should've been feeling before crashes over me like a wave. I want to crouch down and bury my face in Elvis's fur, but I've just gone on a rant about how I'm not immature, so I can't very well pull the "you can't see me if I can't see you" trick. Miriam puts a hand on my back, and I suddenly wonder how I ever managed to stay upright without her.

When I glance at Dad, his face is bright red, and it has such a weird expression on it that I can't even tell if he's angry or upset or embarrassed or what. It makes me want to throw my arms around him and say I'm sorry, that I didn't mean it. But I *did* mean it.

"I can't have this discussion right now," he finally says, and his voice comes out much quieter than I expect. "I need to get out of here."

"David, I think what Ella is trying to say is—" Beth starts, but Dad holds up his hand, and she stops talking.

"You and I need to have a chat," he says to her. "Come on. I'll drive you home."

And then he turns around and walks away from us.

Today, 4:11 p.m.

Me: OMG I can't BELIEVE this whole Aunt Libby/Beth thing

Jordan: I KNOW

Me: SO CRAZY

Jordan: SO SO CRAZY

Jordan: Seems like they're about to break up tho, thank god

Me: Yeah he seemed pretty freaked out by all that stuff about the universe bringing them together

Me: Here's the thing, though . . . she doesn't actually seem that bad?

Me: Like I know you really hate her but I guess I don't really know WHY

Jordan: She just drives me NUTS with all her new-agey stuff

Jordan: She buys me those inspirational posters like the ones outside the principal's office for my birthday

Me: She got me one of those too!

Jordan: And totally disgusting tea that tastes like dirt

Jordan: And she tries to get me to brush my teeth with baking soda instead of toothpaste, so gross

Jordan: And she's always trying to make me quit tae kwon do cause it's "too aggressive"

Jordan: Whenever I say anything negative she tells me to do yoga breathing and put good intentions out into the universe

Jordan: Like, come on, I'm a human! I'm gonna get mad sometimes! It's fine!

Me: Totally

Me: Tbh she did some weird stuff with us too

Me: I really wanted something to work out for my dad so I tried not to think about it

Me: When I fell off my bike, she twirled this crystal over my ankle to absorb bad energy

Me: And she tried to rearrange our furniture when she came over for dinner

Jordan: SHE DOES THAT TO US ALL THE TIME

Me: Like . . . she doesn't seem like a bad person or anything . . .

Jordan: No, she's not. We're just . . . really different

Jordan: I hope she finds a guy with 17 ferrets who makes her very happy

Me: LOL

Jordan: EVGAP sometime this week?

Me: Definitely

Me: I seriously need it

Jordan: ♥

— 20 —

Mom spends the first five minutes of the car ride home snapping
at me to put my phone down and lecturing me about being irresponsible on the internet and trying to manipulate Dad and Beth and "who knows how many other people." Then she spends the next five minutes reassuring me that Dad still loves me even though I messed up. I really can't handle any more feelings right now, so I curl up into a tight ball in the back seat and repeat "I'm sorry," and "I know," and "I really don't want to talk about this," over and over and over. Finally Krishnan tells her to leave me alone, that I'll talk when I'm ready, and she goes quiet and turns on the radio. I spend most of the drive slipping in and out of sleep, lulled by the voices on NPR, having dreams about crowds of people laughing at me.

We stop at a Chinese restaurant on the way, and I eat my pork lo mien in silence. Before we get back on the road, I go to the bathroom and toss my "lucky" watermelon lip gloss in the trash with all the dirty wet paper towels. I never want to see it again.

It's past nine by the time we get home, but I'm wide awake from my car nap. I know the normal thing to do when you've had an awful day is to watch dumb TV or play a video game or read a fantasy book, something that lets you escape from real life. But the only thing I really feel like doing is working on my science fair project. It seems like what happened today with Dad and Beth and losing the dog show was all spectacularly bad luck, but analyzing my data will remind me that nothing is random. Everything in the world happens according to predictable patterns, and if I don't understand something, it's just because I haven't figured out the logic behind it yet.

I hook Krishnan's digital camera up to the computer in the study, and then I play the files one by one in slow motion, holding a protractor up to the screen so I can measure the angle of each tail wag. It takes much longer than I thought it would, but it's soothing to do a straightforward task that doesn't involve any feelings. By the time Krishnan tells me to get off the computer and go to bed, I'm actually pretty calm.

The minute I'm done with breakfast on Sunday morning, I get right back to it. Halfway through the afternoon, I finally pencil my very last number into my spreadsheet, and my heart speeds up. It's possible I'm the first one to ever think about tail wag angles, and soon a piece of life that seemed chaotic and inexplicable to everyone will suddenly make sense.

There are no obvious patterns in the numbers, so I pull out my calculator—when your results hide, it makes it even more fun to dig them out. I average all the tail wag angles for each dog, then calculate what percent deviation each stimulus caused. It all looks pretty random still. I list the tail wag angles for each stimulus in order of the dogs' ages, the owners' ages, the dogs' weights, but I still can't find a pattern.

Mom pokes her head into the study and says Dad has a work emergency. She wants to know if I'd be okay with staying here tonight and there tomorrow instead, and I tell her it's fine. I try not to think about how there's no such thing as a detergent-advertising emergency. I try not to think about how furious Dad must be with me if he's canceling Italian Food Sunday.

I sort the data by the kind of snack I held up, by the kind of toy, by what time I did the tests. I separate the dogs by sex and try everything again.

Hours later, I still haven't found any sort of pattern at all.

Like everything else in my life, my data is a random, chaotic mess.

I'm barely able to pay attention the next day in science. When the bell rings, my friends throw their stuff into their bags, chattering about how excited they are for the pizza in the cafeteria. Keiko pokes me in the ribs as I'm zipping up my pencil case. "Hello? Anybody home?"

"What?" I say.

"I asked you three times what your bet is for what the topping will be today. Jordan and Mir say pepperoni. I say sausage."

"Um . . . ," I say, but I can't focus on pizza toppings right now. "I don't know. Save me a seat, okay? I need to talk to Ms. McKinnon for a minute."

"Okay, sure," Keiko says. Mir shoots me an *Are you okay?* look over her shoulder as she follows everyone else out the door, and I give her a half shrug in reply.

I wait until everyone has left before I approach Ms. McKinnon. Today she's wearing a shirt with two giraffes on it, their necks bent into the shape of a heart, and looking at it makes me feel better for some reason. "Hey, can I talk to you for a second?" I ask.

"Of course," she says.

I pull out my spreadsheet and my notes and hand them to her. "I spent all day yesterday trying to analyze the data for my science fair project, and I can't find any sort of pattern," I tell her. "Will you take a look?"

Most of the other teachers I've had would give my numbers a quick skim and tell me not to give up, to keep on working until I found something. But Ms. McKinnon isn't most teachers. We sit down together at one of the lab tables, and she asks me to talk her through every step of my work, since explaining things out loud can sometimes help you make connections. When I'm done, she takes my spreadsheet and my notes and goes through them carefully, recalculating a few of the percentages to make sure I did them right. Eventually she puts the papers down and turns to face me.

"I'm really proud of you, Ella," she says. "This is some excellent experimental work. Your methods are great, and you've been incredibly thorough. You're becoming such a great scientist."

"What did I do *wrong,* though?" I ask. "Can you just tell me? I've spent *so* much time thinking about it, and I can't figure it out."

"What makes you think you did something wrong?"

"Because this data doesn't *show* anything. I thought my procedure was good, but maybe it wasn't, or maybe I messed up because I was distracted, or maybe—"

"Ella," my teacher says gently, and I stop talking. "Your data *does* show something. It shows that there isn't a pattern."

I stare at her. "What?"

"I mean, we can't say for sure—this is only one trial. To be totally certain, you'd have to test a much bigger sample of dogs, and you'd need to run the experiment a bunch of times. You'd have to make sure other people got the same results when they followed the same steps. But finding that there's no pattern doesn't mean you've done anything wrong. Not every experiment shows how things work. Sometimes they show one of the many, many ways things *don't* work, and that's valuable information too."

I feel like the firm, solid basis of everything I believe is tilting to the side, making it hard for me to stay upright. I grip the edge of the table to try to hold the world in place. "But everything has a pattern. There are laws of science, and everything has to follow them. It *has* to. You told us that."

"That's true," Ms. McKinnon says. "There are laws about motion and thermodynamics and conservation of energy, and on the very smallest level, atoms tend to behave in predictable ways."

I nod hard. "Right. And everything is *made* of atoms, so if each one of them follows set patterns, then shouldn't everything else do that too? I'm not saying it's easy to find all the patterns, but they're still *there*, right? If we dig hard enough?"

Ms. McKinnon leans back in her chair and props her feet up on the metal ring around the bottom. "It seems like it should work that way, doesn't it? Some people do believe it should be theoretically possible to predict the future by predicting the movement of atoms. But a dog isn't just a bunch of subatomic particles. Dogs are living creatures with millions and millions of neurons in their brains, and each of those neurons fires hundreds of times per second. Scientists know a ton more about how brains work than we used to know even ten years ago, but it's still not even the tiniest fraction of everything there is to know. So the fact that you didn't find a pattern doesn't mean you did your experiment wrong. It just means that the ways in which animals express happiness are complicated. Imagine how difficult it is to figure out patterns in the *human* brain—we each have *a hundred billion neurons.*"

I think back through the past couple of months—the way I tried over and over to find the right variables that would make my dad fall in love, the way I pinpointed every problem I could possibly have at a dog show and nipped each one in the bud. I thought I had made things totally foolproof. But I still didn't win the dog show, and my dad and Beth are over almost before they began, and now Ms. McKinnon's basically telling me that even if I had worked much harder, I couldn't have made things turn out any differently. I *couldn't* have read Elvis correctly and adjusted my handling, because he wasn't trying to tell me anything at all. The world doesn't follow rules. It's completely, totally random.

I really don't want to cry in front of my teacher, but the tears spill down my cheeks before I can stop them.

Ms. McKinnon's hand flies up to her mouth. "Oh my god, I'm so sorry. I didn't mean to upset you. If you base your science fair project on this data, you're going to get a really good grade, I promise. You don't have to get perfect results to get an A. It's all about the process, and I can see how hard you've worked."

"It's not about the science fair," I sniffle.

Ms. McKinnon goes to her desk and brings back a packet of tissues, and I take it and pull out three. "Do you want to tell me what's wrong?" she asks. "You don't have to; I can write you a pass to go see Ms. Maciel if you'd feel more comfortable talking to a counselor."

But I trust Ms. McKinnon, and I suddenly find that I *do* want to tell her what's wrong. Soon the whole story is pouring out—my parents' divorce, the way my dad doesn't seem like himself anymore, all the dog show stuff, Head Over Heels, the zoo, getting stuck under the table, the way Beth turned out to be Libby. The only thing I leave out is the way I tried to set *her* up with my dad at the open house. Ms. McKinnon's hand is warm on my back, and it feels good to say everything in order. Talking it all out makes the world stabilize under my feet, and I let go of the lab table.

By the time I'm done, lunch is nearly over, and my tears have slowed to a trickle. "Oh, Ella," Ms. McKinnon says. "You've been going through a lot. Thank you for telling me about it."

I shrug and wipe my eyes with yet another tissue—I've used up almost the whole packet. "Are you going to tell me I couldn't have done anything differently because everything in the world is pointless and random?"

Ms. McKinnon laughs, a sudden, surprised sound. "No, of course not. None of this is pointless at all; it's really important. And it's not exactly random either, though some of it is coincidental, and some of it—like the dog show and the ways people feel about each other—is very subjective. Those are things you couldn't have controlled, no matter what you did. I know it's hard, especially for someone as conscientious as you, but I really hope you can stop beating yourself up about those things."

"I get how falling in love is subjective, but I don't see how the dog show could be," I say. "Like . . . it's about who handled their dog *best*. We all did the same exact procedure. It should be obvious which person did it closest to perfect, right?"

Ms. McKinnon thinks for a minute, and then she says, "You do ballet, right?"

"Yeah."

"Say two professional ballerinas did the same choreography, and both of them did all the steps exactly right, no mistakes. If you asked a whole audience to pick which dancer did the routine better, do you think everyone would choose the same person?"

I shrug. "I don't know. I guess not."

"Why do you think that is?"

I think about something Miss Caroline said at last week's rehearsal for the winter concert. "Because . . . dancing is about more than getting the steps exactly right. It's about the way you feel the music and stuff."

"So each person might look a little different when they do the same choreography, even though each of them is technically right?"

"Well . . . yeah." I suddenly see what she's trying to tell me. "Oh," I say.

"You got it. Now, as for your dad . . ." She sighs. "That's more complicated."

"He's so mad at me," I say, and a few more tears threaten to sneak out. "I wanted things to be better for both of us, and now everything's all messed up, and I have no idea how to fix it. How do I make him—"

"That's the thing about emotions," Ms. McKinnon says, cutting me off. "You can't *make* them do anything, especially when nobody's totally right or totally wrong. It's not an exact science, and there are a lot of things you can't control. But there are also lots of things you *can*." She ticks them off on her fingers. "You can control how honest you are about your own feelings. You can control how much empathy you have for someone else's situation. You can control whether you own up to the mistakes you make and how you express that you were wrong."

Even though her entire point is that emotions aren't like science, it's comforting to hear it broken down like steps in a procedure. "Make things right" seems so huge and overwhelming, but all these smaller steps seem more doable.

I can definitely say I'm sorry. I can tell Dad how I'm feeling and explain what my thought process was, step by step, like how I explained my experiment to Ms. McKinnon. And this time, maybe I can do it in a way that doesn't involve screaming my head off.

"You're a compassionate person, Ella," Ms. McKinnon says. "And I've met your dad—he seems like a reasonable guy. I know you two can find a way forward if you're both honest."

When she smiles at me, my heart feels lighter for the first time in days.

"Okay," I say. "I think I can do that."

— *21* —

I spend the rest of the day nervous but determined, practicing what I'm going to say to my dad over and over in my head the same way I go over dance steps and dog show patterns. But I guess I don't seem very confident on the outside, because Mom takes one look at my face as we pull into Dad's driveway and says, "Sweetheart, are you okay?"

"Yeah," I say. "Why?"

"You look like you're steeling yourself to go off to war." She tries to pull me into a sideways hug, which doesn't really work because of our seat belts. "I know you're nervous about seeing your dad after this weekend. You'll probably need to have some tough conversations. But don't be afraid to tell him what you're feeling. If he and I had been more up-front with each other about how we felt, we might have a friendlier relationship now. And even if you did make some mistakes, the things you said to him on Saturday were totally valid."

"I know," I tell her. "I already know what I'm going to say to him, actually."

"Oh." She looks surprised. "Do you want to do a practice run?"

I shake my head. "I think this stuff should be private between Dad and me."

Maybe that's ridiculous, since I screamed out half of it in front of a whole convention center full of confused strangers, but Mom nods. "That's fair," she says. "If you want to call me later and let me know how it goes, you can. But I understand if you don't."

"Thanks." I lean over and kiss her cheek. "Love you."

"Love you too, Ellabella. See you tomorrow."

I grab my bag out of the back seat, march up to the door with my head held high, and take a deep breath. And then I stick my key into the lock and turn it.

The delicious smell of garlic bread hits me immediately, and I almost start crying before I even *see* Dad; I really love our traditions, and I'm suddenly terrified that things will never be the same between us. Maybe it would be better to take back everything I said and accept all responsibility for being wrong, and we can go back to the way things were.

But I hear Ms. McKinnon's voice in my head, telling me to be honest, to take ownership of the things I can control. The way things are is safe, and I always know what to expect, but it's also exhausting, pretending to be cheerful all the time and dancing around certain topics to protect Dad's feelings. I deserve better than that. We both do.

"Hello?" I call. "I'm here."

Dad comes out of the kitchen in an old Sox T-shirt and his ripped, grass-stained jeans. There's a smile on his face, but it's a strained one that doesn't quite reach his eyes, and he stops short in the doorway, like he's not sure if he should hug me. We stare at each other for a long moment, and then he holds out his arms, and I dive into them.

"Hey, Ellabee," he says, and hearing him say my nickname again makes me feel so much better and so much worse all at once.

"I'm glad to see you," I say.

"Me too. I'm sorry about yesterday."

"I'm sorry, too. About Saturday, and what I said, and so much other stuff, and I—"

He cuts me off. "Why don't you come in? Dinner's ready, and once we have food, we can talk. Okay? I made your favorite Bolognese."

"Okay," I say. Just the fact that he cooked my favorite dinner even though he's mad at me makes me think we might be able to work things out after all.

When I'm settled at the table with a heap of pasta on my octopus plate, Dad says, "All right. I want you to start from the beginning and tell me about this whole dating website situation. Maybe you should start by showing me my profile."

So I do. He reads it carefully on my phone, occasionally wincing or snort-laughing at something I've written, though I'm not sure what's so funny about it. Then he listens as I tell him about Penny and the zoo and about Linda and getting trapped under the table at Little Pete's. ("Wow, everything makes so much more sense now," he says. "I really thought that woman was insane.") I show him the interactions "he" had with each woman, and then I pull up all the texts I sent Beth.

When I'm done, he heaves a huge sigh. "You understand that what you did was really wrong, don't you?"

I nod.

"And you understand *why* it was wrong?"

"I shouldn't have tricked all of you," I say. "None of these women had any idea what they were getting into, and neither did you. It wasn't fair to any of you. I'm sure I hurt everyone's feelings. And people shouldn't impersonate each other on the internet, obviously. That's probably, like, identity theft or something."

"I want you to write e-mails to Penny and Linda and Beth explaining what you did and apologizing for your behavior."

"Okay," I say. "What exactly ended up happening with Beth, anyway? After we left the dog show?"

Dad sighs again. "We, um . . . We decided we weren't really very well suited to each other."

I wrinkle my nose. "Was the ride home super awkward?"

"Pretty awkward, yeah."

"I'm really sorry. I hope I didn't, like, ruin dating for you forever."

"I don't think one failed relationship can ruin dating *forever*. But I probably won't look for someone else right this second. And when I do, it definitely won't be on Head Over Heels. You're going to have to show me how to delete that account." I promise I will, and then Dad is quiet for a minute, rubbing his temples like this whole conversation is giving him a headache. "I just don't understand why you did this," he finally says. "It all seems so . . . *complicated*. What made you think tricking me into dating was the best way to get me to come to your show instead of *talking* to me about it?"

"I tried to talk to you about it," I say. "But I knew you'd refuse to come if it meant you'd have to be in the same room with Krishnan. Every time I even say his *name* you shut the conversation down. And you made it clear that you don't like me doing dog shows. You tried to talk me out of going back after that first one. So I . . . I thought it might be easier for you if you had someone to go with."

"I'm fine with you doing dog shows," Dad says. "I would never try to control what hobbies you pick as long as they make you happy. I wasn't staying away because of that or because of Krishnan. I was trying to give the two of you space to bond."

My brain struggles to wrap itself around this information. "Wait, *what?*"

"You know I talked to Dr. Obasanjo once in a while when you started seeing her after the divorce, right?" I nod. "Well, she told me it was important for me to let you establish a relationship with Krishnan on your own terms, one that was completely separate from me. Dog shows were your thing with him. So I thought it would be best if I stayed away from that whole world altogether."

I blink at him. "So you wouldn't come see me compete because you thought it was *good* for me?"

"Obviously I went a little overboard on the whole staying out of the way thing," Dad says. "But I honestly had no idea how badly you wanted me to come. You never told me how important it was to you.

Why didn't you say something? I would've been there in a second."

And here comes the hard part. *Honest and forthright*, Ms. McKinnon's voice whispers inside my head.

"Sometimes it can be kind of hard to talk to you about stuff," I say.

"What do you mean? We talk all the time."

"We talk, but we don't really *talk*." That doesn't even make any sense, so I take a deep breath and try again. "It's just that ever since you and Mom got divorced, you've been . . . different. Not like your old self at all. You seem, like . . . *faded* or something."

That crease appears between Dad's eyebrows again. "Faded how?"

"Like, you and Mom used to go to parties and shows and movies and host dinners and stuff all the time. And now all you ever want to do is sit around the house and watch baseball and work in the yard. And I read online that decreased activity and pulling away from people are signs of depression, and obviously it's normal to be depressed when you get divorced, so I know it's not your fault or anything. But sometimes I feel like I can't be honest with you about stuff that's upsetting me because you're obviously so unhappy already, and I don't want you to be even *more* upset because you're worrying about me on top of everything else. You know?"

Dad looks *super* upset now, which is exactly what I was trying to avoid. I'm starting to wish I'd never brought this up at all. But then he finally opens his mouth, and the words that come out are the ones I least expect to hear.

"Sweetheart," he says gently, "I'm not depressed. Not at all. I'm so sorry you've spent all this time feeling like you had to protect me, but I'm *fine*. Seriously. I'm happier and more content now than I've been in years."

"But . . . no, you're not," I say. "If you were fine, you'd act like your old self. Mom acts the same as she used to."

"Maybe I'm not acting like my old self, but I'm acting like my *real* self," Dad says. "All those parties and all that hosting? That was for your mom. I did that stuff because she loved it, not because I wanted to. There are lots of reasons the two of us weren't compatible, but that's one of them. Doing that kind of stuff exhausts me. I'm happy to go out sometimes, but watching baseball and working in the yard and cooking for you on weekends is really much more my speed than entertaining. I'm an introvert. Do you know what that is?"

"It means you're shy," I say. "But you're not shy at all. You're super friendly and good at talking to people."

"That's not quite what it means," Dad says. "It's more that I get my energy from being alone. When I've been out socializing, I need to have time by myself for a while to recharge. Your mom is the opposite; when she's alone for too long, she starts to get really lonely and sad. But when you see me sitting quietly and reading or something, it doesn't mean I'm depressed. It probably means I'm relaxed."

I've spent most of the past few days feeling like everything I know has been tipped on its side, and now I feel like the world has rolled over yet again, leaving me hanging upside down. But when I flip back through my memories of Dad with this new lens in place, what he's saying actually does make sense. He has seemed quieter, and he's wanted to stick closer to home, and he's definitely not the snappy dresser he used to be. But I guess he hasn't actually seemed *unhappy*, now that I really think about it. I just assumed he was because he's been acting how I'd probably act if *I* were depressed. I guess I'm not an introvert.

There are so many things to say that I have no idea where to even start. I'm so relieved I haven't destroyed everything between us, and I'm thrilled Dad will come to any event I want if I ask him, and I'm struggling to come to terms with the fact that the guy I thought was my *real* dad may never have actually existed in the first place. It's a lot to take in. I decide to start with, "I'm really glad you're not depressed."

Dad laughs. "Yeah, me too."

"I guess I shouldn't have tried to get you to date," I say. "I thought that maybe if you stopped being lonely, you'd turn back into your old self. But I guess you didn't want to be your old self in the first place."

"I really appreciate that you care about me enough to try to fix me. But I don't need fixing. There are lots of ways to have a happy life."

I know this isn't the most important thing right now, but a question won't stop tugging at the corner of my brain, so I let it out. "Does it make you tired to be with me?"

Dad reaches out and grabs my hand. *"Never,"* he says. "Absolutely not. You're my kid. You're not in the same category as everybody else. Being with you is as relaxing as being alone. I never want you to worry about that."

Something deep inside me releases, and breathing is suddenly a little easier. "Okay. Good."

"I'm really glad we finally talked about all this," Dad says. "And we can talk about it more any time you want. How would you feel about going to see Dr. Obasanjo together a couple of times? It seems like we both have a lot to figure out, and maybe she could help us find some strategies for communicating better."

Going to Dr. Obasanjo after the divorce was kind of hard—she always asked me a ton of questions about things that were difficult to face head-on. But it also made me feel better to confront those things, and I'm pretty sure that's exactly what Dad and I need to do right now. If someone can help things start to feel normal between us again, I'm okay with giving it a try. "I guess we could do that," I say.

He squeezes my hand. "Good. I'll give her a call tomorrow. I want to be the best possible dad for you."

"And I want to be the best possible kid for you."

Dad gives me a real smile for the first time all night. "You already are, kiddo," he says. "No matter how many mistakes we both make, that's never going to change."

To: PennyForYrThoughts,
To: DrownedInMoonlight
To: Sirsasana77
From: SuperDad_DSC

Hi! This is David's daughter, Ella. I'm writing to you from "his" account because I wanted to tell you that I'm really, really sorry.

Each of you has had some pretty weird interactions with my dad over the last couple of months. Please don't blame him if those messages and conversations were confusing and/or upsetting. I'm the one who made this account, not him, and I'm the one you've been chatting with . . . he didn't even know I was doing it. He honestly is a really great guy and the best dad ever, and all the nice things I said about him were true. (For example, he IS really great at making Italian food!) I thought I was doing a good thing by helping him find love, but it was sneaky and mean to mess with your lives, even though it was for a good cause. I'd be upset if someone lied to me about who they were, and I should've thought of that much sooner. Like, *before* I did it.

Anyway, all of you seem really great, and I'm sure there are tons of guys out there (who aren't twelve-year-old girls pretending to be guys) who would love to go on dates with you! Maybe some of you have found The One already. . . . I really hope so! And if you haven't, I hope you do soon.

Sorry again, and please forgive me!

Sincerely,

Ella

— 22 —

Two Sundays later, I tell my dad I have a surprise for him.

We get in the car, and I program the address into my phone so the GPS can guide us to the right place. "I appreciate that you agreed to come out with me today even though you don't know where we're going and you'd probably rather stay home," I say, because Dr. Obasanjo told us we should use positive reinforcement to let each other know when we've handled situations well. That made sense to me right away; it's like giving treats to Elvis when he follows a command.

"I appreciate that you appreciate it and that you're telling me so," Dad says, and we both snicker, because even though it's helpful, the whole thing also feels a bit ridiculous.

Dr. Obasanjo is actually the one who sparked the idea for today's surprise. She suggested that Dad and I find a new activity we can do together, something that will build trust. At first she wanted us to go to a climbing gym, but Dad shot that idea down immediately, which was the right call—he would probably fall off the wall in five seconds and throw his back out, and that wouldn't help anyone. He came up with a plan to teach me guitar so we could play duets and sing together, and I still want to do that too. But this is even better. I know Dad's going to love it, and Dr. Obasanjo's going to be super proud of me for thinking of it.

We pull up to the bright blue house with the white shutters, and I say, "This is it, right here. You can park in the driveway."

Dad does, and we pull in behind the red hatchback that's already there. "Whose house is this?" he asks.

I smile mysteriously. "You'll see."

He turns off the car and stares me down. "You're not trying to set me up with another woman, are you?"

I snort. "This is way better than a girlfriend. Just wait."

Anjali opens the door the second I ring the bell, like she was waiting for me. "Ella!" she cries, pulling me into her arms. "How are you, babe?"

"Good," I say. "This is my dad, David. Dad, this is Anjali. She's Krishnan's sister."

A guarded look comes over Dad's face, but he holds out his hand to Anjali politely, and she shakes it. "Krishnan's not here," I say. "Don't worry, that's not the surprise. Come in."

I struggle out of my purple puffy coat, and Anjali takes it, along with my dad's green parka. "You can go on back," she says to me with a wink, and I don't have to be told twice. I take Dad by the hand and pull him through the yellow living room, down the orange hall, past the coral bathroom, and open up the door to the purple study.

"Dad," I say, "meet Minerva and her puppies."

Minerva's sprawled out on a huge dog bed in the center of the room like a queen on her throne; she yawns in my direction as she nurses three of the puppies. Another one is sniffing around under Anjali's desk, trying to figure out a way to tip over the heavy trash can, and the fifth one—the *best* one—is by the couch, gnawing on a plush squirrel toy and trying to show the world how incredibly fierce she is. She has on the purple collar I got her.

"That's Molly, Luna, and Neville," I say, pointing to the nursing puppies—they all look kind of the same, but I could tell them apart right from the very beginning. "That one over there with the white feet is Albus. And *this* is my Hermione."

I scoop her up and kiss the heart shape on her velvety head, and she wriggles and licks my nose until I squeal. "Who's a good girl?" I ask in that stupid voice that automatically comes out of your mouth whenever you see a baby animal. "Who's the best girl? Is it you?" Hermione makes a tiny high-pitched squeak—her attempt at barking—and it's so ridiculously cute that I can't even deal.

I offer her to my dad. "You want to hold her?"

Dad's eyes are all soft and melty, and he immediately reaches out to take the squirming puppy from me. "Oh my god, she's so tiny," he says as he cradles her in one arm, and Hermione's tail goes nuts as he scratches her belly.

"She's the cutest dog in the world, right?" I ask.

Dad rubs one of her ears between his fingers, and Hermione pushes her tiny nose into his hand and licks his fingers. "I've seen a lot of cute dogs," he says. "But I've gotta say, this might actually be *the* cutest dog in the world."

"So, um . . ." I bite my lip and twist my hoodie sleeve around my finger, suddenly nervous. "Do you think you'd maybe want her to live at your house, when she's ready to leave Minerva in another month? I thought it would be cool if we could take her to obedience classes and teach her tricks together. And maybe she'd be good company on the days I'm at Mom's. She wouldn't expect you to talk if you wanted to be all introvert-y."

It's like Dad's eyes light up from the inside; I can't remember the last time I saw him this excited, and I can tell he's completely head over heels in love with my dog already. "Really? You don't want to train her with Krishnan? I thought he was supposed to be the expert."

"I don't need an expert," I say. "I'll ask Krishnan for tips if I need them, but I really want to do this with you. If that's okay."

"That's . . . that would be more than okay. I would love that." Dad holds out the arm that isn't holding my dog—*our* dog—and I snuggle up against his side, making a Hermione sandwich. She squeaks again and chews on the drawstring of my sweatshirt, but she doesn't seem to mind so much.

Anjali comes in and laughs when she sees us all huddled up together. "I see Hermione made a new friend," she says.

"He said yes!" I tell her.

"I'm not surprised. Who could resist that face?" She claps Dad on the shoulder and says, "Congratulations, Papa. She can go home with you guys after New Year's."

Dad smiles down at Hermione, and then he beams at me, and

when he says, "I can't wait," it seems like he really means it.

Anjali reaches in and gives Hermione a good scratch behind the ears, and her back leg paws the air like crazy. "It's too early to tell for sure, but I think she's going to make an excellent show dog. Great coloring. Good bone structure. If you start training her early, she can enter her first competition when she's six months old. You may have a winner on your hands."

Part of me thrills at the prospect, and my head floods with images of parading around the ring with my perfect dog, who does exactly what I want without even having to be told. I picture myself collecting ribbon after ribbon, making it to the finals at the National Dog Show or Westminster.

But then I think about all the things Ms. McKinnon and I talked about the other day. I could do everything exactly right and never win a single show. I could spend countless hours training Hermione and never achieve that mind-meld I want. She's a living creature with millions of neurons and her own personality, not an experiment I can control. And if I'm honest with myself, maybe training her to stand still for a judge and run certain patterns flawlessly isn't the most fun thing I could be doing with her. It's possible I liked the idea of bending everything to my will until I won better than I liked the actual competing and practicing. Hermione and I could stand in a ring every weekend, rigid and well-behaved . . . or we could spend that time playing Frisbee and rolling around in the dirt, wild and free and chaotic, without any rules hemming us in.

Just like Dad told me, there are lots of ways to have a happy life.

After trying to control everything for so long, it's scary to let go of the reins. The hardest thing in the world for me to do is nothing. But maybe for once it might be best to step back and let the unexpected in.

"Ella?" Anjali says again. "What do you think?"

"I'm not sure," I say. "Maybe someday, when she's grown up. For now I just want to . . . see what she's going to become, you know? It's a total mystery, and I'm not sure it's right to try to control her. I think I should let her be who she is."

Anjali looks confused. But my dad locks eyes with me and smiles, and I know I've said the right thing.

The two of us—the *three* of us—are going to be okay.

ACKNOWLEDGMENTS

Infinite tail wags of gratitude to the following people, who were instrumental in the creation of this book:

My editor, Amy Cloud. Amy is my Saint Bernard, the ultimate rescue dog renowned for its soundness of mind. Whenever I get stuck, she's there to dig me out of the snow with her insightful notes and friendly encouragement.

My agent, Holly Root. Holly is my Border collie, tirelessly herding humans and contracts and payments without letting a single member of the flock stray. Collies are known for their ability to work extremely long hours on uneven terrain, which is pretty much the definition of a good agent.

My beta readers: Lindsay Ribar, Michelle Schusterman, Jen Malone, Heidi Schulz, and Claire Legrand. These women are my standard poodles, a breed renowned for its extreme intelligence and general delightfulness as companions. I don't know what I'd do without them, as a writer or as a person.

My whole team at Aladdin, who makes my books look gorgeous and works so hard to release them into the world. They are my Siberian huskies, the sled dogs who function seamlessly as a group and always get their cargo to its destination safely.

Angela Li, my cover artist. Angela is my German shepherd, a breed lauded for its hard work and boundless adaptability. This is the third cover she has drawn for me, and the style is always just right for the substance.

My copy editors, Kayley Hoffman and Beth Adelman. Copy editors are the terriers of the publishing world, working long and hard to catch and kill all the vermin in a manuscript. There's not a single rat left in this book because of your handiwork.

Steve Berns, Joseph Ingram, and Tricia Ready, my Chesapeake Bay retrievers. Chessies are known for their helpful nature during hunts and search and rescue missions, and these three friends fetched me so much invaluable information about dog shows and spaniels.

Melissa Sarno and Renee Lasher, my Cardigan Welsh corgis. Corgis were developed to be companion dogs, and Melissa and Renee kept me company at the Westminster Kennel Club Dog Show as I took endless notes and petted endless furry heads.

All my incredibly supportive friends, my Cavalier King Charles spaniels. These dogs are often called "comforter spaniels" because they're so devoted and loving. I needed a *lot* of support and encouragement while writing this book, and they were always there for me.

Susan Cherry and Erica Kemmerling, my family and fellow red-haired Irish setters. These dogs are known for being sweet-natured, active, and independent, and if that doesn't describe these two women, I don't know what does.

And last but not least, George Harrison, my favorite Welsh springer spaniel. (This one's literal.)

If you liked *Ella Unleashed*,
turn the page for a peek at Alison Cherry's
Willows vs. Wolverines.

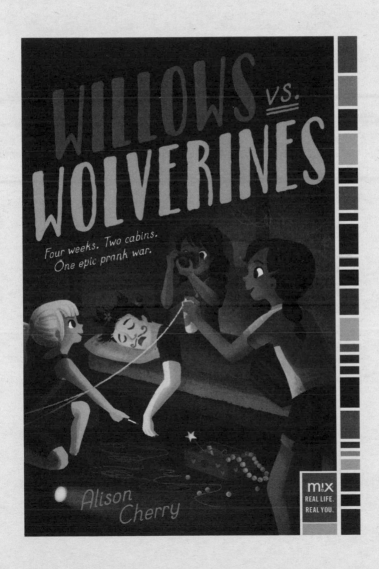

Mackenzie and I are on an ugly orange bus filled with strangers, and all of them are singing off-key.

"Foxtail, Foxtail, burning bright, you're my heart's one true delight!" shrieks a chorus of piercing voices, and I slump farther down in my ripped vinyl seat, hoping some of the sound waves will fly over my head and miss my ears. I don't understand how anyone could be so excited about Camp Foxtail. Then again, the rest of these kids probably don't know what they've been missing at Camp Sweetwater, where Mackenzie and I have spent summers since we were eight. And where we *would* be headed right now, if there were any justice in the world.

"No singing until we're on camp grounds!" shouts the driver. He's got about twelve pieces of gum in his mouth, so the words sound garbled, but his exasperation comes through loud and clear. I can tell he'd rather be doing pretty much anything other than chauffeuring a bunch of kids to middle-of-nowhere Michigan—going to the dentist, shoveling snow, getting all his leg hair waxed off.

I know how he feels. This is the last place I want to be too.

Mackenzie rubs her eyes under her purple-framed glasses. "I can't believe we're missing Midnight Snack at Camp Sweetwater," she grumbles.

"I *know*," I say. "I've been dreaming about it all year." After the Welcome Campfire there was always this enormous late-night snack buffet in the mess hall—sundae ingredients, popcorn, cookies, you name it. Mackenzie couldn't eat most of it because of her dairy allergy, so we invented these special dessert sandwiches made of toaster waffles, peanut butter, bananas, Marshmallow Fluff, and chocolate syrup: the ChocoNanaFlufferNutter Delight. We've tried to replicate them at home a million times, but they never taste the same. Mackenzie once read about this Chinese restaurant that put drugs in its disgusting food so people got addicted and kept coming back, and we have a theory Camp Sweetwater might do the same thing with their peanut butter. We even pooled our allowances and bought a drug-testing kit so we could investigate our hypothesis this summer. I wasn't exactly looking forward to peeing in a cup in the spider-filled cabin bathroom, but I was totally prepared to do it for science.

Of course, that was all for nothing now that my parents and Mackenzie's had some stupid falling out with Delilah, their friend who runs Camp Sweetwater. Why do adults have to be so dramatic about their friendships? Don't they realize camp is way more important than whatever they're fighting about?

"I bet Camp Foxtail won't even *have* peanut butter," I say.

"They'll probably feed us eggplant casserole and chicken feet and those disgusting Jell-O molds with canned fruit that my great-aunt Doreen makes," Mackenzie says.

"They'll probably make us eat dog food." All this talk of food reminds me of the package of Red Vines in my backpack, so I dig it out. Mackenzie takes a whole handful. There's not much that can improve this situation, but candy makes everything at least a *little* better.

"I bet the lake will be full of seaweed and trash and leeches," she says with her mouth full. "I bet we won't even be able to swim."

"I bet they won't have *beds*. We'll have to sleep on the floor."

"Or on the lawn."

"Or in the *woods*."

"Or in a *pit of snakes*."

"And what kind of name is Camp *Foxtail*, anyway?" I ask. "It's like they were too cheap to name it after an actual animal, so they named it after a piece of fuzz hanging from an animal's butt."

Mackenzie finally cracks a smile. "Camp Fuzzbutt," she says, which makes us both start giggling. At least she's with me on this horrible orange bus. There's no way I could make it through an entire month of this horror show without her.

The ride takes four hours. By the time we finally turn onto the dirt road marked with a huge wooden sign in the shape of a fox, I'm restless and cranky and thirsty from all the sugar I've eaten. The second we bump past the sign, everyone starts scream-singing *"Foxtail, Foxtail, burning bright"* again, and this time the driver lets them get all the way through it. There are only about three other people on the bus who don't seem to know the words, and despite the fact that I don't want to be here, I feel left out.

I know I should feel lucky that I get to go to camp at all—none of my aunts and uncles went, and they won't let my cousins go either, even though they've been begging for years. The rest of my family thinks my parents are totally nuts for letting me go away for an entire month, but my mom has all these amazing memories of spending her summers at Camp Pine Needle in Minnesota, and she wants me to have similar experiences. Then again, if that's the case, she should really send me to a camp where I'll actually have *fun*. I wish more than anything that Mackenzie and I were riding through the familiar arch that marks the boundary of Camp Sweetwater right now, belting out the Sweetwater Anthem Delilah taught us when we were little kids.

The bus winds through the woods, and I brace myself for what I'm going to see when it pulls out the other side. I know how much photos on websites can lie. But the woods open up onto a wide green lawn, and then the bus lurches to a stop in front of an old-timey-looking wooden building. There's a sign that says FRIENDSHIP SOCIAL LODGE above the front door, which is super cheesy, but the lodge itself actually looks pretty nice.

I turn to Mackenzie. "Hey, do you think—" I start to say, but she's staring out the window in the other direction.

"Whoa," she says quietly.

My eyes bug out when I see what she's looking at. I knew Camp Foxtail was bigger than our old camp, but I didn't realize it was *this* much bigger—there are easily *two hundred* kids on the lawn. I knew practically everyone at Camp Sweetwater, but here I don't recognize a single face.

At school, I'm never the most popular or the best at anything—Dani Alvarez and Nick Riccardi get the highest grades, Sasha Hollingsworth always beats me on swim team, and Lily Greer-Whipple is the teacher's pet. I'm not even the class clown—Gavin Yeh's jokes are *so* dumb, but the whole sixth grade still thinks he's the funniest. But at Sweetwater I was always the pranking queen. Dozens of girls always swarmed me the second I got off the bus, eager to hug me and take selfies with me and hear about the hijinks Mackenzie and I had planned for the summer ahead. Camp was the only place where I was cool and interesting and fun without having to try.

Now I'm going to have to start all over again at the very bottom of the social ladder, and just thinking about it is so exhausting that I want to cry. Nobody at this camp even cares that I'm here. It might be *forever* before I have a solid group of friends. For all I know, it might not happen at all.

I'm about to complain about all of it to Mackenzie, but before I can say anything, she reaches out her pinkie finger. It's our secret signal for "I need moral support," and I realize how terrified she must be right now. The first day of Camp Sweetwater was always hard for her even though Delilah was there, so I can only imagine how she feels surrounded by strangers in this brand-new place. I shouldn't be thinking about making new friends when the best friend I already have needs my help.

I link my finger through hers and hold on tight. "It's gonna be okay," I say. "We can get through anything as long as we're together, right? Even leeches. Even *eggplant casserole*."

Mackenzie shrugs and says, "I guess," instead of smiling like I'd hoped, but when the girls in front of us get up and push toward the bus doors, she lets go of me and stands up too, so I guess maybe I helped a little. I stay right behind her as we climb off the bus so she knows I have her back.

A counselor in a bright orange T-shirt that says I'M FOXY across the chest is standing at the bottom of the steps with a clipboard. "Name?" he asks.

"Izzy Cervantes."

He traces his pen down the page until he finds my name, and I see that I'm listed as Isobel, which I hate. The counselor makes a neat check mark on the paper and smiles at me. "Have a great summer, Isobel," he says, and then his eyes skate right past me and onto the next boy. If this were Camp Sweetwater, Delilah would be rushing over right now to welcome Mackenzie and me and sneak us some of the sour candies she always carries in her pockets. It's so weird and sad to be just another couple of names on a list.

We must be the last group to arrive, because I'm not done gathering my duffel and my sleeping bag before the counselors start blowing whistles and herding everyone into one big group in the center of the enormous oval-shaped field. There's a flagpole at one end and soccer goals at the other, and the cabins are spaced evenly around the edge. Camp Sweetwater only had twelve cabins, but here I count twenty. Mackenzie sits down all the way at the edge of the group, and I join her, though I always prefer to be closer to the center. I look around and guess which of the other girls might be in our cabin, and when I spot a couple of friendly-looking ones our age, I try to make eye contact. But they're busy talking and showing each other pictures before their counselors make them put their phones away, and none of them notice I exist. I tell myself it's not an omen for how the rest of the summer will go.

Another counselor in a FOXY shirt gets up in front of the group. "Who is stronger than an ox?" she shouts.

I barely have time to shoot Mackenzie a look like *What?* before everyone on the lawn shouts back, *"I am! I am! I'm a fox!"* They're all holding up three fingers next to each temple, which I guess is supposed to represent fox ears.

"Who here thinks outside the box?"

"I do! I do! I'm a fox!"

"Who's as steady as the rocks?"

"I am! I am! I'm a fox!"

"Who's more graceful than the hawks?"

"I am! I am! I'm a fox!"

"Dumbest chant *ever*," Mackenzie grumbles. "How is a fox stronger than an *ox*?" I know she's thinking about the cheer she made up last year that became part of the standard Camp Sweetwater repertoire; it's so sad to think of our friends singing it around their Welcome Campfire without us. But even though the fox call-and-response is way stupider than our old cheer, part of me wants to join in, just to be part of the group.

I'm about to make fox ears with my fingers like everyone else, but the chant is already over, and the counselor shouts, "Welcome back, campers! Who's ready to have an *amaaaaazing* summer?"

Everyone screams, and I feel stupid sitting there in silence, so I clap. Mackenzie keeps her hands folded in her lap.

"Let's get started, then! First, I'd like to welcome all our brand-new Foxes! Raise your hand if this is your first summer at Camp Foxtail!"

A bunch of hands go up, but almost all of them belong to little kids, and for a second I'm not sure what to do. I don't really want to call attention to the fact that I'm an outsider, in the same category as a bunch of eight-year-olds. But at the same time, I *do* want everyone to notice I'm here. So I put my hand in the air and smile to let the other campers know I'm friendly. Mackenzie glances at me, then looks at the ground and raises her hand to shoulder height.

"How about a big round of applause to make them feel welcome?" the counselor shouts, and everyone claps. "Perfect! We're so glad to have you all with us, and we know you'll love Camp Foxtail as much as we do! And now . . . are you ready for some *cabin assignments*?"

Everyone screams again, and the counselor starts calling out names, starting with the littlest kids. The wide-eyed third graders follow their counselors to their cabins, lugging their too-heavy bags behind them. One tiny girl sitting near us starts crying when her name is called, and an older boy who has the same dark hair and eyes wraps an arm around her shoulders. "Don't be scared," he says. "You're going to love Cottonwood Lodge. That's the one I told you about with the purple door, remember? Maybe later today you can help your counselor teach your cabin all the Camp Foxtail songs you know. That would be cool, right?" The little girl nods and wipes her eyes, and when her counselor beckons her over, she puts on a brave face and goes.

It's stupid, but for a second I wish I had a big brother to hug me and tell me everything's going to be fine. I'm twelve years old, and I should be able to take care of myself. But no matter how brave you are, it's nice to have someone to show you the ropes when you're in a new place. When you're the oldest kid in the family, you always have to figure everything out for yourself.

At least Mackenzie and I have each other. I nudge her with my shoulder. "You want the bottom bunk again?"

"Yeah," she says, and she gives me a tiny smile. I start looking forward to tonight after lights-out, when we can whisper together until we fall asleep. One of the best things about camp is that it's like having a four-week-long sleepover party with your best friend.

The kids who are getting called now look about our age, so we start listening for our names. The boys' cabins are all named after woodland animals—Badger, Chipmunk, Raccoon, Owl—and the girls' cabins are named after trees—Cottonwood, Birch, Poplar, Cedar. Mackenzie's name is the third one called for Maple Lodge, and I grab my backpack and get ready to stand up too. *I'm a Maple,* I tell myself, and I try to feel some pride in that—cabin loyalty is a big deal. I wonder what our cabin cheers will be like. I can't think of anything that rhymes with "maple" besides "staple."

But then the counselor finishes reading off the names of the Maples, and I realize I haven't heard mine. I probably wasn't paying enough attention. "She called me, right?" I whisper to Mackenzie, but then I see that my best friend's eyes are wide and scared. She shakes her head.

"But how is that possible? They can't put us in different cabins. They must've made a mistake, right?" Mackenzie's only six weeks younger than me, and we've never been in different cabins before. We've never been apart for *anything* at camp; Delilah always made sure we were in the same activities and on the same team for capture the flag and the Sweetwater Olympics. We were together so much that everyone referred to us as IzzyAndMackenzie, one word.

A short counselor with a black ponytail raises a hand above her head and shouts, "Follow me, Maples!" and girls start making their way over to her. But Mackenzie's still standing next to me, staring wildly around like she's forgotten how to walk. I'm upset, but she's clearly full-on panicked. If she had known we'd be separated, I doubt she would've agreed to come to Camp Foxtail at all.

"You should go over there," I whisper, and I try to keep my voice as calm and brave as possible. "It's okay. We'll still see each other all the time, right?"

"I guess," she says, but she doesn't sound convinced. We both know how much time everyone spends with their own cabins.

I link my pinkie with hers and give it a squeeze. "Go," I whisper. "I'm sure they're all really nice. I'll see you at dinner, okay? And in the meantime I'll talk to someone about getting you switched into my cabin." No matter how miserable Mackenzie is, she never makes a fuss, so fixing this will be up to me. Not that I mind helping her, obviously.

Mackenzie nods. She takes a deep breath, and then she turns and walks away, head down, her purple-sneakered feet dragging in the dirt. I try to keep a reassuring smile on my face in case she looks back at me.

But once she's out of sight and I'm left alone with a bunch of strangers, I suddenly don't feel very brave anymore either.

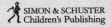

Be sure to M!X it up by catching up on the latest drama!

Real life. Real you.